"Everything Good ain't God"

2

PRODUCT
OF MY MOTHER'S
Pain

TAMARA S. LAGUINS

ISBN-10: 978-1-943409-79-2

www.purethoughtspublishing.com

Printed in the United States of America

Table of Contents

Dedication

To my Lord and Savior, Jesus Christ, I can do all things through you, but without you nothing that is made is made, so apart from you I can do nothing. You have given this to me, and I pray that, in your eyes, this glorifies you. Thank you for loving me beyond my flaws and for your gracious and merciful forgiveness. You and You alone are AWESOME.

To my husband, you are still P.U.S.H.ing me. Your encouragement is priceless. Thank you for asking questions that motivated my thoughts and for giving me the room to "sit down, get that laptop, and write" and to "save it, put it away, and rest." I love who God created you to be in my life and the bond that He continues to strengthen between us. Forever is a long time, and forever is who you are to me. I love you, "Forever".

To my awesome supporters, you know who you are, a big THANK YOU!!! I thank you for the phone calls, the text messages, the Facebook posts, and the free promotion (LOL). I THANK YOU for the phone calls threatening me to get on with the second part and the trillion questions that inspired direction in this writing process. I thank you for the testimonies that you shared with me and for sharing the impression that this book made on you. WE all have a story! The word of God teaches us that we overcome the enemy, the same that seeks to steal, kill, and destroy, by the Blood of Jesus and our testimony of Jesus Christ. Don't be afraid to share your TRUE story! Just be sure that you share it with integrity at the right time to the right people with the right motive; God will help you with that.

To my children, God blesses us with dreams and equips you with all you need to make them come true. Follow your dreams, and let nothing and no one stop you! I love you more!

I love all of you so very much, and there is nothing that I want to change about that!

Dr. Tamara S. La Guins

Chapter 1

LADY LORNA J.

Once a First Lady, Forever a First Lady

It seemed like it was just yesterday. Once again, Lorna had awakened sweating with tears running down her face. You would think that after thirty-one years she would be passed this, but how does one get past the unresolved murder of a loved one? Counseling? Forgiveness? Lorna wanted what she felt she deserved; sweet revenge. Her husband, a well-known pastor of a flourishing congregation and prestigious following all over the country, was her pride and joy. He was about to go to a higher level when someone maliciously, and without thought of his family, gunned him down at their very front door. Lorna would never forget that evening.

The day started off as a really exciting day for Lorna. She had finally convinced him to take some time off to go to a doctor's appointment with her. She knew he was in for a surprise. Lorna already knew in her heart of hearts that she was pregnant and had three tests to prove it. Not only had she been earnestly praying like Hannah in the Bible, but she had also been flushing her birth control pills away. She wanted *his* baby. Even though they had been married for ten years, her husband, Pastor James Caleb Hewman, pastor of Holy Ghost Fulfillment Baptist Church, insisted that it was not the right time for them to have a baby. He would attempt to reason that God was increasing his territory, and he needed to be focused and centered at all times to operate as God wanted him too; that was where she came into play. As his wife, J.C., as she called him in private, expected for her to be ready at a moment's notice to make appearances by his side or entertain major entities in the religious arena. That's why he sent her to the beauty and nail salons every two weeks like clockwork; he even made the appointments. She had only canceled one appointment in the 10 years she had been married, and she learned very quickly that this was unacceptable and would not be tolerated. James was the head of their home and would not accept what he perceived as challenges. Other than his temper, he was a good husband and dynamic pastor. She knew he would be an awesome father once he looked into the face of his little mini-me. He would come around when the doctor told him he was going to be a father in the upcoming summer; so she chose to believe.

Lorna was far too cautious of upsetting him to attempt to sneak a pregnancy test in their home, but she had taken the tests when he allowed her to visit her sister for the weekend. He wanted to give his undivided attention to the Birminghams whose son had just died while serving in the army. His step-mother seemed to have taken it very hard and insisted that she and Brother Birmingham receive counseling from J.C. Lorna was elated when he called and told her to just stay at her sister's home for the weekend because he was going to be busier than he expected with the Birminghams. She had been talking with her sister about missing her cycles and tiring from trying to keep it hidden from J.C. She had been wasting money buying sanitary napkins, along with her usual monthly hygiene products, and discarding them as if she had used them. It was truly an exhausting charade. Once she received the permission to stay, Lorna and her sister raced down to the local Walgreens Pharmacy and bought three pregnancy tests. She was right! She was pregnant; all three tests confirmed it. She had to be at least three months which meant she would have her husband's seed in the summer. Lorna was elated!

Truth be told, J.C. did not allow Lorna to stay with her sister out of the kindness of his heart; he needed her out of his way. Bro. Birmingham had already canceled the counseling appointment scheduled. Just as J.C. was reaching for the phone to let Lorna know she had been with her sister long enough, Sis. Birmingham strolled into his office wearing another short low cut dress and sat down in one of the chairs in front of his desk. After clearing his throat, J.C. decided to inform Sis. Birmingham apparently of what her husband had not.

"Uh-um. Good evening, Sis. Birmingham. That certainly is a beautiful dress you're wearing", J.C. had to force himself to stop staring at the glowing peak of her thighs.

"I thought Bro. Birmingham would have told you that he canceled the counseling session this evening. I was actually about to call Lady Lorna and head out," he was hoping that she would take the bait and leave before what he was truly thinking became obvious.

"Well, Pastor, I was hoping you could counsel *me*," she began to sob and blow her nose. "See the death of my stepson is really taking its toll on my marriage. Charles has not touched me at all since it occurred. We used to have such an intimate relationship; always hugging and kissing like teenagers. Lately, he just sits in front of the television and drinks all day and all night until Sunday comes. I think he only comes to church out of habit or because he doesn't want anybody to suspect rising trouble in our home."

J.C. was attempting to stay in his pastoral mode but could feel his flesh weakening. Clearing his throat again, he hoped what he said next would convince Mrs.

Birmingham to go home and seduce her own husband.

"Sis. Birmingham, now, I have noticed the smell of alcohol on Bro. Birmingham, but I didn't want to come down too hard on him because I know this loss has to be tough on him. You know he was a widower when you met him, right? Everyone grieves differently and heals at individual paces."

"I understand that Pastor, but I am a woman with more time behind me than ahead of me. I have needs and desires", she began as she patted her revealed cleavage with her crying towel as if it were 100 degrees in the office. "My husband is selfishly inconsiderate of this even though I have been right there with him through the entire situation. I cry at night too, but it would be a lot easier to bear the pain in the arms of a man," she looked at him with a solemn face as if to say she needed *his* arms right now.

J.C. knew *he* needed to get *her* out of his office quickly before he gave in to temptation. She was more deceitful than she was beautiful, but she was clearly all woman. At that moment, that was good enough. Why was he being tempted like this? Amid his thoughts, he heard her sobbing again. He justified himself with his next thought. He was her pastor; it was his duty to provide her comfort.

He finally stood up from his chair and walked around his desk. Grabbing Kleenex with one hand, he extended the other hand to Sis. Birmingham. As she quickly took his hand and stood from her seat, J.C. pulled her to him and gently wiped away her tears. She laid her head on his chest, and knowing what she wanted, he wrapped her in his arms and held her. The longer he held her, the tighter his embrace became as they stood in his study. She finally looked into his crystal brown eyes and kissed him passionately. Before he could break away, he was returning her kiss. The only thing that stopped the lustful escapade was the knock on the door and the sound of Sis. Good's voice calling for him as she always did when she was done with her cleaning.

"Pastor?" She never waited for his response. She entered the study and could immediately tell she had interrupted something.

"Pastor, I'm done with my cleaning and headed out. I best be getting home before my chillun' get to worrying about me." Sis. Good made her way between the guilty parties. "I know you can't wait to get home to that pretty wife of yern. You been waiting on me long enough, so Sis. Birmingham can walk on out with me. I'll see that she gets on off the premises safely." Sis. Good firmly gripped Sis. Birmingham's hand and pulled her toward the study door. "Goodnight, now."

As they walked out, neither woman had any words for the other. When they were outside of the church, Sis. Good finally cut through the tension that thickened between them.

"I have to lock up. I'll watch you get to your car and drive away. Have a good night, Sis. Birmingham, and tell Bro. Birmingham we say hello."

Sis. Birmingham stomped off as she spoke her reply, "I'm not the one you need to watch, Sis. Good. When I see Bro. Birmingham, I'm going to say a whole lot, but hello is not a part of it."

Sis. Good sat in her car on the opposite side of the street until she saw the pastor exit from his study and drive off towards home. She had been praying about his lusting after the flesh, and there was plenty of willing flesh amongst the congregation. Sis. Birmingham was a fool if she thought she was the first. Sis. Good knew that Lady Jay had a good heart, though she could be manipulative and often overlooked the reality of a situation as if that would change the outcome of it. She guessed it did change things in Lady Jay's mind. What Sis. Good did not know was that J.C. had picked up the phone to call his wife. Only this time it was to tell her to stay where she was because he had more intensive counseling to do. He had also called the number Sis. Birmingham had slipped on the desk behind him as she was dismissed by Sis. Good. It said to call her for a follow-up, so they scheduled a counseling appointment for the following day at another location.

When Lorna returned that Sunday, she had already made an appointment for Tuesday morning. She practically begged J.C. to go with her as she spoke with him on the drive home. When she entered her home, she was greeted with the usual church hug and cordial good evening attitude, but she refused to allow it to ruin her mood. She took a relaxing bath as she rubbed the small bulge of her belly. By the time she exited the bathroom, J.C. was sound asleep. She crawled into bed, feeling relaxed and excited about Tuesday.

It seemed like Tuesday took forever to come, but that morning she had ironed J.C.'s baby blue shirt and navy suit with his pink tie and handkerchief. She dressed in a baby blue floor-length, high-waist maxi dress. She put a pink flower in her hair. As usual, they complimented each other by all appearances.

While waiting in the patient room for the obstetrician's return, J.C. became kind of quiet. He seemed very nervous and irritated. Before she could say something to calm his nerves, Dr. McQuary entered the room.

"Well, Hewmans, you're about to bring another little "HEW – MAN" into this world! Congratulations!!!" He laughed heartily at his own joke. Lorna saw the frown form across J.C.'s brow, but she did not want to draw the doctor's attention to it.

Lorna squealed with delight as she pretended to be surprised. J.C. looked stunned and angry. Without so much as a 'thank you', he walked out of the room. How had this happened? Well, he knew, but this was still totally unexpected! After, the doctor gave his dos and don'ts, Lorna was allowed to go. Walking alone to through the parking lot, Lorna knew it was going to be more difficult than she thought to change her husband's perspective. He never had a good father growing up and never wanted to be a father as an adult.

Lorna's excitement began to diminish on the way to dinner. J.C. did not utter one sound throughout dinner and all the way home. Upon their arrival, J.C. got out of the car and left her sitting there. Usually, he opened her door for her, but this time he walked to the front door without looking back in her direction. Entering their home, she could no longer stand the silent treatment.

"J.C., please say something to me. We're about to be parents. Are you not just a little bit thrilled that YOUR seed is being nurtured and prepared? YOUR bloodline will carry on, Sweetheart." Lorna was holding her breath as she waited for a response.

"To answer your question, Lorna, no, I am not a little bit thrilled my seed is being nurtured and prepared because anything that is to come from you is NOT of God!!!" JC was literally spitting the words in her direction. "The deception was conceived in your mind long before a child was conceived between us; therefore, it is stolen. The Lord revealed your manipulation to me even before we wed, but I did not see the desperation you harbored."

"Stop it!!! Stop it!!!!" Lorna felt something explode inside of her. "How dare you self righteously stand there and read me like I am beneath the ground you walk on? I may be deceitful, manipulative, and even desperate, but one thing I am not, dear husband, is STUPID."

Her mind was telling her to stop; to leave it right there. Her heart was speaking and would not be silenced. She married a man just like her father; charming, calculated, cold, and without remorse. She married a man that wanted fame and flunkies and found both in the church. Her husband, like her father, saw women as possessions to be dressed up, used, and tossed away.

"Do you think I don't know about the women you have "counseled" after hours? Do you think I don't know why so many come and so many go when they realize that they were simply temporary satisfaction for a terminal problem?" Lorna could no longer quench the fire within her. "Unlike you, I knew exactly WHAT I married, and don't you forget that I also knew exactly how to get you where you are today! You don't know God any more than the flunkies you entertain, so cut the act. YOU may not want this baby, but you are going to put on the hellacious act that you have become so good at over the years. Smile, Husband, because we are your pride and joy!"

By the time it was all out, and the "bad girl" appearance had subsided, she was winded. She did manage to make one last statement as she walked toward the stairs,

"James, I am still going to help you grow. Now, this baby will allow me to love you even if you don't love me. We will be the perfect family."

As she began to make her way upstairs, she heard the doorbell ring, but she never looked back to see who was on the other side of the door. She always regretted not being able to look at the murderer in their face. As she reached for the doorknob of her bedroom door, the noise rang out. She knew they were gunshots. She raced down the stairs, and before she completed the trek, she could see J.C. lying on the floor of the foyer.

She knew before she reached him that he was dead.

As she ran to the door, she saw a woman in a hooded coat and a long black dress or skirt walk into the woods on the side of their home. Lorna turned her attention to J.C. He had been hit by all three shots. She was not sure how close the shooter had stood or if they had a deliberate aim. Later, the coroner's report showed exactly what she had seen with her own eyes. J.C. had been shot in the head; the heart; and the groin area.

Just like that, Lorna was a widow. Her dream of a picture-perfect family had been shattered by a devil in a red covering. She knew she could not stay in that country little town with her dead husband's harlots whispering behind her back. She knew they would be laughing at her demise, while those that knew about J.C.'s infidelities would pity her. She would not have either. Only two other people knew she was pregnant: one was her loyal sister and the other was dead. Lorna decided to take her husband's body back home. Despite what she knew of him, she wanted him to be laid to rest surrounded by people that loved and respected him, and she refused to allow his death to tarnish her entire reputation or that of her family. The day she followed behind the car that held her husband's remains did she come face to face with his killer. Lorna burned with vengeful desire as she watched the girl in the red coat walking toward the Mitchell home.

The timer on the stove woke Lorna from her flood of memories streaming from her nightmare. As she prepared her warm milk, Lorna smiled. She knew it would not be long before her nights would be of peaceful rest. J.C.'s murder had become old news, but retribution had not been obtained. She wanted those that were closest to her shattered dream to fill the pain she had carried for so long, and she had raised her child, unknowingly, to want the same. The generation of past sins would have to suffer. Turning the lights down as she returned to her bedroom, Lorna settled into her rocker with her cup of warm milk.

She began to rock as she hummed her favorite song, "You don't know; you weren't there. You don't know when, and you don't know where. You don't know what the Lord told me."

Chapter 2
CARRINGTON
Mother Knows Best

On days like this, when the sky was overcast with a little sun peeking through the breaks in the gray clouds, Carrington sat on the back patio of the home that now belonged to her and James and starred up towards heaven, the hills, and out across the lake. This was her place of solitude. The place where she often sipped her hot tea as she examined what life had quickly become for her.

Her mind drifted back to the very night she left her mother's house. She could still see the silhouette of her mother's frame in the window. She could still feel the piercing brown eyes staring out at them as they sped off into the night. Why had she disobeyed her mother? She always thought highly of her mother and respected her mother's uncanny wisdom. Carrington felt convicted in her spirit before the car even

know where. You don't know what the Lord
told me."

Chapter 2
CARRINGTON
Mother Knows Best

On days like this, when the sky was overcast with a little sun peeking through the breaks in the gray clouds, Carrington sat on the back patio of the home that now belonged to her and James and starred up towards heaven, the hills, and out across the lake. This was her place of solitude. The place where she often sipped her hot tea as she examined what life had quickly become for her.

Her mind drifted back to the very night she left her mother's house. She could still see the silhouette of her mother's frame in the window. She could still feel the piercing brown eyes staring out at them as they sped off into the night. Why had she disobeyed her mother? She always thought highly of her mother and respected her mother's uncanny wisdom. Carrington felt convicted in her spirit before the car even moved, but James wasted no time. Taking her by her hand, he drove off as if her mother was hot on their trail. It surprised Carrington that her mother did not attempt to stop them. She didn't race to the door and out on the porch, and yet, Carrington felt her presence.

That night they drove all the way to his house. James was like a kid filled with Christmas-like excitement on the whole drive home. He talked about how perfect life was becoming and the plans that he knew God had drawn out for them. He didn't seem to notice her silence or her sweaty palm he was holding. Carrington wondered how he could be so sure of what God had planned for them when everything in her was crying out that this was wrong. This was not what, who, when, or how God intended for things to be. Was it her consciousness or her mother's voice in her head? She didn't know if he ever stopped talking, but so many thoughts were spinning through her head she felt dizzy and soon drifted off to sleep.

"Carrington, wake up sleeping beauty. You are home", James whispered softly in her ear. "I allowed you to sleep while

I unloaded the car. You need to go upstairs and take a nice hot bath so that you will be ready for dinner by seven."

Carrington was a little taken aback by his use of the word "allowed". As he spoke, he helped her out of the car and escorted her towards the house. Just after her feet crossed the threshold, he spoke his final note of instruction for the time being.

"Please, don't be late. Tonight is a very special night." He kissed her on her forehead and disappeared from her sight into another room.

The most delicious smells were coming from the kitchen like someone was preparing a feast. Carrington didn't ask any questions; mainly, because she was afraid of the answers. She did as she was told and walked upstairs to the bedroom. Entering the bedroom that she had slept in as a guest made her tingle with nervousness. She was no longer a guest; she was home. So why did she feel so out of place?

As she sank into the hot suds that filled the tub, her body gave way to the exhaustion she had been trying to fight. She didn't realize how the time was passing by until she was startled by the knock on the bathroom door. Oh, my! Was James about to walk in? She was not ready to be naked in front of him! Carrington had not thought about the next steps they would take once they had arrived at his home; their home.

"Carrington?" a woman's voice called.

That certainly wasn't James.

"Mrs. Shaw?" Carrington answered with confusion. Why was she here, and how did she know Carrington would be here?

"Honey, are you alright? I knocked on the bedroom door but became concerned when you didn't answer."

Still wondering why she was here, Carrington finally got her thoughts together enough to respond.

"Yes, I'm fine. I guess the drive caught up with me. I'll be out in a second." She attempted to sound relaxed.

As she exited the bathroom, Angela Shaw was standing in front of the vanity table holding a garment bag out towards Carrington. Nervously giggling, Carrington walked toward her and took the bag. Angela reminded her of a high school girl eager to dress her for some big date. Whatever it was that was about to happen, it was obvious that Angela had more information about it than Carrington.

"I hope you love it! Just from visiting with you last time, I got a sense of your style. I was so ecstatic when James told me what you were doing and asked for my help. Please....hurry, open it!" Angela began to giggle with a hint of her own nervousness.

Holding her breath, Carrington, gently laid the bag across the bed. The last time she was in this room, James had surprised her with a beautiful gown. Why was this gown so important that he enlisted the help of the professor's wife? What was she talking about when she said: "what they were doing"? So many questions whirled around in Carrington's mind that she forgot to breathe. She almost fainted when she unzipped the garment bag and pushed the sides open to reveal a beautiful pure white wedding gown.

"Oh, Honey! Are you alright? Here let me help you sit down." Angela helped Carrington to the vanity table.

As Carrington sat down facing the mirror, she looked at her reflection starring back at her. What had she done? What was she doing? Was she ready for this? She knew the answers to all of these questions, but she was finally free from her mother's shadow. It was time for her to be the grown woman she gave the appearance of being. She wanted James, and he definitely wanted her. She was sitting in *her* own home. She was about to become Minister James Calvin Reaper's wife; however, the fact that she had defied her mother still weighed heavily on her.

Angela interrupted her thoughts by brushing her hair. "Carrington, you have the most beautiful hair. James told me to tell you to wear it up tonight. We better start getting you ready so that we are not late."

"I can't leave my groom waiting, now, can I?" Carrington knew she had made this bed, but she was not going to lay in it alone. "Yes, let's get this process started. I want my husband to be pleased."

Three hours and twenty minutes later, Carrington stood in front of the full-length mirror in the walk-in closet dressed in her wedding gown. She always thought she and her mother would have the experience of shopping for such an occasion. They would make a day of it. Breakfast, and then, a full day of trying on beautiful gowns. She would know when she found her dress because her mother would be speechless and tearful. Her mother would walk her down the aisle and pass her on to her husband; mother-approved.

That dream was a childhood dream and one that was forever out of reach. Angela knocked on the door to let her know that James was ready. As she followed Angela from the bedroom, the sounds of Luther

Vandross's silky voice floated up the stairs. "If this world were mine......" The lyrics wrapped around her heart and squeezed everything she felt for this man out into the open. She wanted James more than she wanted to breathe. Soon, she would have him. Angela led her to the patio door. Before she opened it, she told Carrington that she would go out first, but Carrington was to follow the roses to the lake.

"Carrington, you are a beautiful bride. I wish your parents could have made it back in time to witness this moment."

Wait. What? Again, Carrington had no clue what Angela meant by what she was saying. Back from where? What had James told her and Professor Shaw? She didn't have time to think about that now. She made a mental note to speak with James about lying on her parents later not knowing that what was unfolding would soon have her forget all about this little fabrication. Hearing Luther fade-out, she knew the change to Stevie Wonder's "Ribbons in the Sky" was her cue.

As she stepped out on the patio, she took in the scene around her. There were hanging lamps everywhere that made the night glow around them. Pink, yellow, and red roses lined her white rose petal column aisle. She took her time making her way toward the lake. When she looked up, she looked right into James' face. The vision was surprising, but made the anxiety she felt fade away. James had completely shaved his head and goatee. Carrington could see his strong jaw line and luscious lips. He actually looked younger, but still ever-so sophisticated and sexy. Their eyes met, and a slow smile formed across his handsomely chiseled face. It was only when she got closer that she realized he was not looking at her.

When Carrington made her way beside him, she followed where James' attention had been as his bride walked down the aisle. Professor Shaw was officiating, and his wife, whom Carrington assumed was asked by James, was standing as Matron of Honor. There was only one guest in attendance. She was a strikingly beautiful well-dressed woman Carrington had never seen before. Even in the romantic lighting, Carrington could see that her makeup was flawless. Not a hair was out of place, and she held a posture that commanded she be noticed. Who was this woman that James seemed to be even more enamored with than her? Carrington tried to be respectful and gave a little smile, but the woman seemed to completely ignore her and kept her gaze on James. Professor Shaw began to speak to signify the beginning of their ceremony.

James and Carrington stared into each other's eyes as Professor Shaw led them through the traditional vows. This was another disappointment to Carrington though she dare not let on. She always envisioned she and her husband-to-be would speak from their hearts or read heartfelt vows that they had each written for their special moment. She quickly dismissed her emotions as she understood that the ceremony was simply a formality. The marriage is what is most important and must be given the most effort and attention.

"I, now, pronounce you husband and wife. James, you may now salute your bride," pronounced Professor Shaw.

Carrington closed her eyes and waited for that magical moment that always transpired when James kissed her. She felt his strong hands gently cup her face. She could smell his breath so she knew it would be any second. Then, she felt a simple peck from his lips and it was over. Suddenly, James was embracing her in his arms. Was it over all ready? What was that?!

"Carrington, open your eyes, you're embarrassing yourself", James whispered in her ear.

Was this what her dreams of a romantic wedding ceremony had been minimized too? A wedding evening planned by strangers, orchestrated by her groom, and then criticized like a silly school girl as she waited for what all brides waited for after taking vows? As Professor Shaw made the pronouncement of their union and her new name, as if there were more than the five people there to witness, Carrington felt that drop in her chest she usually felt when she was hurt and disappointed. To add insult to injury, as she and her new husband begin their walk back toward the house, James actually reached out for the strange woman. Carrington could not believe this foolishness! This woman eagerly took James's arm and walked with the two of them up the aisle as if they were following the yellow brick road straight to Mr. Wiz! Sooner rather than later, the fuming Caring was going to need an explanation about this woman.

When they entered the house, the sounds of jazz engulfed the atmosphere. Carrington didn't realize how hungry she was until they entered the dining room. There was a spread laid out as she had never seen before. James left her standing just shy of the entrance while he escorted the woman to the head of the table. Carrington did not know who she was but could tell she was somewhat older than her own mother. This must be James' mother. Why didn't he introduce them before all of this, and why was he catering to her like this on his own wedding day? The woman had not yet made any gesture to speak to her at all. Carrington already knew they would never be close. All she could think about was her own mother. The mother she left standing in the dark. She had to turn away before anyone saw the tears welling up in her eyes. Professor Shaw and Angela came in behind them and took their places. James encircled her and came to a stop behind Carrington and kissed her neck.

"I want my wife by my side as close as possible and as often as possible." He traced the length of her arm with his fingertips to her hand and led her to the seat on his left side as he took the other end of the table.

The kitchen staff had been hired and began to serve everyone. James was the first to break the silence at the table as the kitchen staff was finished.

"Everyone, I know you are wondering who this stunning woman is joining us on this extremely special occasion. It is with great honor and respect that I introduce to you: *the* Lady Lorna J. Reaper. My amazing mother."

James was obviously very proud of his mother. One thing was a fact: she was stunning. The years seemed to have been good to her. She had to be at least 15 years older than Carrington's own mother, but she was just as alluring.

Before anyone could respond, Lady Lorna J. took the floor.

"My son is too kind. I would not have missed this for all the tea in China. Carrington, James is my pride and joy, and I know that you will see well to his happiness." It was more of a subtle command rather than a compliment, and Carrington caught it quickly.

"I will do my very best; I assure you", Carrington humbly responded. She did not want to rock the boat that seemed to be tilting already.

"Yes, you will. Just take your cue from me, and you will be just fine. I know my son better than anyone with the exclusion of God. Trust me, Carrington; I was well trained by the "mothers" of the church. I know your kind, but I'm going to train you well. Just remember, Love, Mother knows best." Never taking her eyes off of her daughter-in-law, Lady Lorna took a sip from her glass.

James sat there with this sick boyish grin on his face. Professor Shaw must have felt the tension or a little uncomfortable because he spoke a little louder than usual.

"Please, allow me to make a toast to two of my best students and our good friends. We wish you a lifetime of love and happiness. All glory to God!!!"

Everyone toasted except Lady Lorna J. What was with her? Carrington couldn't understand how James could flaunt his mother who did not seem to have an ounce of joy in her concerning his new wife. Carrington had a feeling Mother Dear was going to be making her presence felt quite regularly.

After dinner, The Reapers, including Lady Lorna J., said their farewells to The Shaws. Carrington did not know why, but she hated that they were leaving. Perhaps it was the fact that she would now be left alone with Lady Lorna J., and James, she suspected, would be of no help. She closed the door and turned to face The Lady and her son, but they had already begun to ascend the stairs.

"James", Carrington tried to sound like the sweet needful wife.

"I'm just taking Mother to her room and saying goodnight, Carrington. Please wait for me in your room." He never even looked back to give her orders, but Lady Lorna J. didn't miss the opportunity to turn and give Carrington a sadistic smile.

It was not the least bit cold in the house, but Carrington could not deny the chill she felt all over her body. She picked up the train of her dress and climbed the staircase alone. This was definitely not how she ever imagined ending her wedding night. As she entered *her* room, as James called it, she continued to hold back the urge to cry. She knew what she needed, but was not sure how, or even if, her mother would receive her call.

James entered the room without as much as a respectful knock.

"Carrington, I came to tell you goodnight, Love. Do you have everything you need?" He really sounded sincere; like the James that she knew.

"James, what is going on? I'm confused. Why are you speaking as if this is not our wedding night?" Carrington just wanted to understand. "Is this not *our* room now?"

"Carrington, Honey, I understand this is our wedding night. Was it not everything you dreamed it would be? Mother spared no expense. I am your husband, and you are my wife. I love you."

James took her into his embrace and kissed her with the passion from their very first kiss. She decided to do what she had never done before. This was her husband, and she wanted him to know she was completely his and only his. James would be her first love and lover. Carrington turned her back to him and began to slowly unzip her dress.

"Carrington, stop that! What are you doing?" James yelled like she was tearing her gown apart. Carrington spun around as much as the train of her dress would allow her too.

"What is it? What's wrong?" Carrington was even more confused than before.

James was already at the bedroom door. He looked very frustrated and slightly disgusted. He wouldn't even look at her.

"Carrington, I thought you understood being I didn't try to sleep with you when you visited. I truly love you, and I am very happy that you are my wife; however, there is something that you must understand and accept. I am and will continue to be celibate." With that, her new husband practically ran out of the room without even closing the door.

This could not be happening. Why didn't he ever say anything? She thought he was simply showing himself to be a true man of God by not pressuring her for sex or attempting to seduce her. What about a family? She needed her mother so badly right now. Carrington just wanted to go home, but what would that prove? Lady Lorna J. was indeed right about one thing; Mother knows best.

Carrington took one last look out at the lake before taking her tea back into the house. As she looked around this cold quiet atmosphere, she could not believe that she had lived here for five years sleeping in the guest bedroom. She was still just a guest in James's home. At 30 years old, Carrington had yet to know what a wife feels like when she makes love to her husband. She didn't know what it felt like to lay in his arms at night after a long day away from him. She was clueless about how it felt to share sexual intimacy with the man that made her his wife. She knew God, for reasons she could not even understand, was still gracing her with His strength. He had helped her to be faithful and be a good wife for five years; however, she did not know how much more she could take. There was only one thing she could think of to do. She couldn't stay mad at her only child forever. Carrington raced up the stairs to her room. She locked the door behind her just in case Lady came over for another unannounced visit. Carrington surmised the mothers of the church never taught Lady that you should knock on closed doors before entering. Carrington sat on the side of the bed facing the window. She said a quick prayer for courage and guidance for her words. Then, very slowly, she dialed home. She needed her mother.

Chapter 3

Tilda

First Appearances & Shocking Revelations

Tildy had really been seeking the Lord about Carrington every day after she crept away with that foul image of a man. She knew the day would come when she would have to let go of Caring, but not like this. Her only child had run away from her home like a thief in the night. WHY? Tildy didn't know what infuriated her the most: the fact that Caring had just run away in the middle of the night or the fact that Caring had defied her for a man! It wasn't just any man either. It was a man that Tildy did not know and did not trust. There was something awfully familiar about him. When she thought "awfully", she meant something sinister. From the moment she laid eyes on him, Tildy felt something wrong. She could not put her finger on it, but she knew there was a bad spirit connected to him. She only hoped that it was not working through him to attack her baby. She prayed that it was not trying to use Caring to hurt her. She could never forgive herself if anything happened to Caring because of her. Despite the circumstances that surrounded Caring's conception and birth, Tilda loved her daughter more than life itself. Caring was the one and only person she would go to Hell to protect. She just hoped this James character understood that, and if he didn't know, Tildy knew she could and she would teach him.

Every day after Tildy finished her duties at the church and told Pastor she was leaving for the day, she came home and grabbed the cordless phone. She carried it all around the house with her as she did her chores and prepared dinner for her husband. She knew her child, and Tildy was determined to answer when she called. She had kept the same routine for five years. With the upgrade in technology, Tildy even bought a cell phone and was able to get calls that came to her home routed to her cell phone. It wasn't that she didn't know where

Caring was living. Tildy's reach was farther than most suspected.

She was so angry the night Carrington left that she couldn't think straight. She wanted to burst into her room and confront her when she heard Caring moving around. She knew she was up to something. Tildy made sure to turn off every light outside of Caring's door, and she waited quietly in the living room. Her blood was boiling by the time Caring made her exit. She didn't even have to go to the window when she saw the approaching headlights go black as a car crept into her driveway. Tildy knew who it was, and who masterminded this defiant plan. She sat so still in the dark that Caring never looked in the corner of the room where she kept her rocker. When Caring walked out of the house, Tildy moved to the window. She watched as the Devil's spawn clawed for her daughter's luggage and hurried her inside of his cage. Tildy felt remnants of who she used to be rising within her or was it that who she was had not changed, but had been suppressed for many years beneath consistent medication and religious activity. She stared so intently at James that she could see a nervousness rise inside of him, and just as she willed, he turned toward the window. Tildy was sure that he saw her, and that is exactly what she wanted. They stood there frozen for a moment in time; eyes locked. A slow evil smirk came across his face. He honestly thought he had won. It wasn't until she felt the corners of her own mouth turn up, that his smirk slowly fell and a second of fear told on him. Yes, he saw her clearly. He slammed the trunk closed and ran to the driver's side of the car and sped out of the driveway like a bat out of hell. 'Little boy' thought Tildy. There are only two things that can defeat evil: a greater evil or God Himself. Tildy knew this battle would determine which side she belonged too.

"Larain, I'm home, Baby." Pastor always came home looking for his wife. Everything in hand was left at the front door until he had laid eyes and a kiss on her.

"I'm in the washroom, Pastor." Tildy had thought about how dirty James was for so long that she went and found a load of clothing to wash. She even stood there and watched the suds turn darker as the unseen grime from the clothing came out.

"Larain, Baby, I thought you just washed clothes this weekend. What are you doing?"

Pastor kissed his love and gave her a hug. She saw the look of concern on his face when they parted. She turned back to the washing machine hoping he wouldn't notice the phone on her hip, but who was she fooling, Pastor noticed everything about her.

"Larain, I see you been carrying the phone, again, today. Are you alright?" He truly asked out of concern.

Pastor knew his wife was hurting and angry, and that was dangerous for all involved. He had never seen the side he heard stories about from the family; some funny and all shocking, but he knew that his wife could be someone to reckon with when all games were put aside. She had been doing well in dealing with her anger and temper until Professor Reaper showed up. Pastor didn't know what it was that Professor Reaper reminded his wife of, but he knew it was not good. From the moment they met, Larain had an extreme enmity for the man. The only thing she would tell Pastor is "there something rotten about him". It had been five years since they had last seen the step-daughter he saw as his own. He missed her so much and had offered to go in search of her just to see if she was alright, but Larain told him no. She seemed to be sure that Carrington would find her way back to them, and she carried home and cell phones day and night.

Larain had no doubt that her Caring would find her way back to her regardless of how good life was with James. She knew that Caring was married to James and living in this beautiful home on a lake. James was the breadwinner, and Larain figured, he wanted it that way. Caring was completely dependent on him so he thought. Larain had been saving money for Caring since she was a baby. Every time one box became full, she would buy Caring a new pair of shoes and take the shoe box and bury the full one in the back yard under her rose bushes. One day

Caring saw her burying a shoebox and questioned her.

"Mama, why are you burying my shoebox?" Caring asked inquisitively.

"I'm sowing your seeds, Caring. One day it will be harvest time, and you will reap your reward." Tildy responded as she continued scooping the dirt back in the hole.

All Caring had to do was make the phone call, and she would have a $15,000 new start. She didn't have to come back home; she just needed to get away from him. Tildy didn't tell Pastor what she had learned, but she did tell him enough to keep him from running out to find Caring.

Tildy had been in the street for a long while, and contrary to popular belief, she had made more than enemies. She was loyal, and even when she began to work on her relationship with God, she didn't judge those still in the street. She was still loyal. She paid light bills; she fed the homeless and less fortunate; she sat in hospitals; she even kept children. They all knew loyalty was a must, so when she went calling, they answered.

Dominic Lamont was the one Tildy called on for the job. He was also her cousin. Dominic looked like a classic businessman and could fit into many circles. He used to be a huge drug dealer in and outside of the area. After a long stint in federal prison, Dominic returned home and came straight to the church. He testified that God was the only one that kept him safe from himself, as well as many other enemies when he was locked away. Everyone he went in with was dead; killed on the inside. Dominic never sold drugs again, but he was still a businessman. He graduated from college while he was put away and earned a business degree. He knew he would catch it trying to get employed when he got out so he says God prepared him while he was inside to use his entrepreneurial skills for a good cause. From an offshore bank account, Dominic put $10,000 into a security business and had accounts with prominent businesses throughout the state and surrounding states. A couple of well-known housewives and once jilted spouses also were happy patrons of his services.

Tildy called on Dominic the day after Carrington had run off with James. She explained that she just wanted to know where she went and what was going on with her. She expected monthly updates unless there seemed to be an emergency, and then she wanted to be alerted immediately. She also wanted to know more about this phony professor. Dominic knew not to waste Tildy's time and jumped on it free of charge. Tildy had made sure that his children, all fifteen, were cared for appropriately and kept eyes on his money while he was locked up. He was forever indebted to her and knew not to play with a woman as determined as Tilda Larain. He had never heard Ms. Tilda threaten anyone, but there was just something about her that said you didn't want to cross her.

Thanks to Dominic, Tildy had gained a lot of information she knew she would need one day, but she knew there were more missing puzzle pieces. She knew James was born and raised in Bay City, Michigan by his aunt and uncle who were pastors of a small church. They had another son named Silas who was about a year older than James and was also in ministry: children and teen outreach. James and Silas never got along, so James left as soon as he could and went to Libertine to escape. He seemed to want nothing else to do with his family. There was a woman that James stayed in contact with who traveled from Michigan to his home at random times during the year. He assumed it was his mother. Four years in and Dominic had not yet cracked the code on this one, but Tildy needed to know so she paid a visit to the Libertine campus herself.

Tildy didn't want to run the risk of James or Caring recognizing one of her vehicles so she rented one when she got to Michigan. Pastor knew she had gone on a girls' trip, but thought she was in New York, and well, she did go to New York with her best friend, Vicki, for a day of shopping. Vicki was always down to handle business. She loved Caring almost as much as Tildy did and would do anything for her best friend and god-daughter. They bought wigs, sunglasses, hats, and other supplies necessary to disguise themselves when they went to investigate for themselves.

Vicki and Tildy weren't just close because they were alike. Tildy trusted her and knew Vicki was smart. She didn't have to spell out everything for Vicki or watch her back with her. Vicki respected where Tildy was spiritually. She also knew Tilda Larain wasn't anything to play with, and she loved that too. They had become fast and close friends when they were both young single mothers. Vicki had grown up in rougher conditions, but despite the things she had endured, she had a good heart. She was a year older than Tildy though everyone that saw them together assumed Tildy was older. It didn't bother Vicki though because there was no competition between them. That was her sister, and that was all there was to it. They met in the hospital after they both had there one and only babies. Tilda had Ms. Carrington and Vicki had Master Tobias Kaneon Oustan or "TKO" as he was nicknamed, and for good reason.

Tildy introduced herself to Vicki as they stood outside of the window looking at their babies. Both had asked the nurses to take their children but wanted to take a peek at their little futures.

"Hey, I'm Tilda Mitchell. That's my baby girl in that awful pink hat right there. I'm 12."

"Hey, I'm Victoria Oustan, and I'm 13. That's my baby boy right there beside your baby. Now, I see why I was in so much pain. Look at the thang!" she laughed at her own joke. Tilda knew she was crazy and liked her already.

"Her name is Carrington Rebekah Mitchell. I named her Rebekah after my mama. She's going to be strong like me and Mama. I just like the sound of Carrington, plus it felt like I was carrying-a-ton while I was pregnant!" Both girls cracked up as they stood in the hall.

"Tobias is the Greek form of the name Tobiah. I found it in a book I stole from the library. I stole it because the lady kept staring at me while I was there, and then, had the nerve to question my reading ability. I left a note that said 'If you can read this, you forgot to ask if I had a library card. Have a good day'!" Tildy howled!

"Girl, you crazy! I like the way you handle yourself though. What does Tobias mean?" Tildy thought it was a beautiful name for the little boy who was indeed a whopper and had just as much hair as Carrington.

"It means "the goodness of God". Ain't that something?" It almost seemed like the young mother was reminiscing about something. Tildy wondered what would have made a thirteen-year-old girl choose such a name. She was curious about this Victoria Oustan.

"Yeah, it is. What made you name your son that?" she had to know.

"Because God is the only good thing I've had in this life of mine. He's the only One I can count on. I believe He's the only reason I'm still here. My baby is living proof that God's goodness is with me." Victoria became real quiet after that. She looked like her mind was taking her on a journey that all led up to this moment.

After a few minutes of complete silence between them, Tildy asked, "Do you want to come to my room and talk some more?"

"Sure."

That was the beginning of a 31-year friendship. That night they talked about the circumstances surrounding their pregnancies. Tildy couldn't tell her everything, but she did confide that she wasn't thinking about sex or babies. She told Victoria that the man that had impregnated her was mean, and no longer around because of what he had done to her. It wasn't until she found out how Victoria had to live that she understood why she found it so easy to talk to her. Tildy had a traumatic moment that left scars. Victoria had a traumatic life that was still an open wound.

Victoria True Oustan was also born to a young girl. Her mother was a prostitute. Vicki's mother had died giving birth to Vicki, and Vicki's father hated her for it. Money became tight on one income being that Victoria had 7 other siblings; she was number eight. It didn't help either that her father was a gambler and an alcoholic. When Victoria had turned 10 her father gifted her to a bookie he owed. She was raped and returned home. Six of her brothers escaped their troubled life by running away. The one right above Vicki, Michael, attempted to take Vicki with him, but her father and eldest brother jumped him before they could make their getaway. To make them stop beating him, Vicki promised to stay home. Her eldest brother was his father's son and to make Daddy happy, he brought money home. Daddy didn't really care where it came from as long as it kept coming. Had he cared, her father would have known that William had been selling his sister to whatever despicable worm was willing to pay, and she wasn't the only one. He had others, willing girls, selling themselves too, but he seemed to take pleasure in humiliating his sister. Vicki had been sold to so many men by this time that she did not know who had given her Baby Tobias. One thing she did know was that she was not returning to that house with her son.

There was an elderly lady, Ms. Agnes; Vicki would go sit with that lived near her family. She told Vicki that after her baby was born, they could come and live with her. She had always been kind to the woman. She helped her carry her groceries; clean her house; and just went over and kept her company. Ms. Agnes truly enjoyed having her around. When she realized that Vicki was pregnant, she demanded answers. Of course, Vicki made up a story to keep the woman from snooping, but Ms. Agnes opened her home to her just like she opened her heart. After learning each other's story, the girls made a vow to one another to always be sister-friends no matter what happened, and that vow had been kept for the entire 31 years.

Tildy and Vicki sat in the rental car outside of what appeared to be an expensive boutique near the Libertine campus. According to Dominic, the mystery lady was visiting and Carrington always brought her to this boutique when she was in town. Tildy was nervous to see her daughter for the first time in five years. She and Vicki had agreed she should stay in the car and listen to the wiretap Vicki was wearing, thanks to Dominic. Tildy was still nervous about what Carrington would look like. Would she recognize her baby?

"Tildy, is that Carrington's car?"

Vicki was referring to a black Bentley trimmed in silver just like Dominic had described.

"Yes, that's it. Here we go, Girl. Watch your sister work!" Vicki seemed just a little too excited as she sucked in her belly and flipped the hair of her wig like some sort of celebrity. She exited the car and made sure to walk right in front of the parked Bentley as she made her way into the boutique. Tildy said a quick prayer knowing her friend all too well.

"Lord, please let this store have something to her liking at a reasonable price and be in her size so this woman won't start flipping over merchandise and hollering about size discrimination! I do not want to go to jail today. In Jesus's name, I pray. Amen." Tildy turned the already low playing radio completely off so that she could hear everything.

When Tildy looked up from the radio, she could not believe her eyes. It was as if she was looking at a younger image of herself. Same brown skin. Same long thick hair. Same curves. How had she missed the woman Carrington had become? Especially seeing that Carrington had become the spitting image of Tildy herself. Carrington was so beautiful, and yet, she looked so miserable in the company of this woman.

Tildy could tell the woman was in her mid-to-late fifties, but she was fit and moved well. She could tell this lady was very confident in herself from the way she carried herself. She looked like she wore and carried labels...real labels. Tildy was sure Vicki would confirm or deny this assumption when she returned. She turned her attention back to her daughter. Why did Caring look so defeated walking just a step behind this woman? Why did this woman seem so familiar? Tildy hoped Vicki could give her some answers when she returned. She began to recite Psalm 23 and pray. She always did this when she could feel stress moving within her. She did not want to think something terrible could be happening to her daughter even though she knew this James was a terrible mistake. Deep in prayer about Caring, Tildy did not realize how much time had passed by until she said Amen. Thirty minutes had passed, and Vicki was still inside the boutique. Tildy did not understand why she wasn't hearing anything. She wanted to go get her before Vicki blew both their covers, but she knew no disguise could hide her from her own child.

Fifteen minutes later, Vicki emerged walking just like the mystery woman or at least attempting too. Tildy was cracking up with laughter when she unlocked the door for her.

"What's so funny, Tildy?" Vicki asked with a serious look on her face. She had no clue how she looked imitating this woman.

"You looked a hot mess walking across the parking lot. Why were you walking like that?" Tildy was still laughing with tears running down her face. "Oh, and did you forget to turn the wire on!"

"Is this thang on?" Looking inside of her blouse, Vicki spoke into her breast. "Oh, Sis, I guess I did. But, Girrrrllllll, that's how you walk when you black and rich! Forget the tap. Homegirl got the money! They know her by name!!! Cute little blonde girl in there said hello and then told me to tell her if I needed help. When Mystery Lady walked in, that girl almost jumped over the counter to help her!" Vicki did her best properly spoken English imitation of the assistant. "Oh, Lady Lorna J., welcome, again, ma'am. The items you inquired about are in your favorite dressing quarters. Please follow me. Tildy, the little girl forgot I was even there!! She left me in a little bitty dressing room like she didn't hear me saying excuse me, a little help please."

"Vicki, why did you need help anyway?"Tildy knew this was going somewhere crazy.

"Shugga, I got stuck in a real nice blue chiffon blouse. I'm calling the woman to help me before I a-fist-ti-ate, and the dog-gone child keep hollering back, "Ma'am, I'm with a very important customer right now. I'll be with you momentarily". Like she just knew I was broke."   Tildy had a look of confusion all over her face, and somehow, she knew this was NOT where the story ended.

"Guhlllllllll, when I came out of that dressing room, you know it was ON AND POPPIN'! I told that heffa I was going to make a complaint about this little ruler bouquet concerning size and social economy decriminalization!!! I pulled every blue blouse I could find off of the rack while she chased behind me trying to pick'em up. That's when little Miss Mysterious came running from the back with her nose so stuck up it touched her hairline."

Vicki sat back pouting and breathing like she had run a marathon. Tildy loved this girl, but it was no doubt in her mind that Vicki was crazy.

"Vicki, it's rural boutique and discrimination; Fix Jesus. Well, did you recognize her? Did you see Caring?" Tildy needed to know who this woman was that was so close to Caring so often. Before Vicki could answer her concern, sirens could be heard and sounded like they were getting closer.

"Tildy, we got to go!!! Hurry, Girl, I can't get another strike!!" Vicki was panicking and wrapping a scarf around her head and face so that all you could see was her sunglasses.

As Tildy wheeled the car out of the parking lot and in the opposite direction of the sirens, she prayed a silent prayer of repentance, and one of thanks that she had let Vicki put black duct tape across the license plate when they arrived at the boutique. She knew it was time to return this car and head home. Not hearing sirens anymore, Tildy felt the eagerness to know more about the mystery lady. Vicki must have read her mind and sensed her desire because she began to speak.

"Tildy, um, about the mystery lady." Vicki was hesitant because she really did not know how her friend was going to react to this newly found information.

"Yes, Vicki. What about her? Do we know her?"

"Tildy, I could be wrong because it's been years since we last saw her. She …..well, she looks…"

Why was this girl stuttering?! "Vicki, just say it! She looks like who?" Tildy was tired, hungry, and losing patience.

"She looks like Pastor Hewman's wife!" Vicki could see the shock and horror come across Tildy's face.

The car ride to the rental facility and the flight home was drastically different from the way the ladies started. Neither woman had much to say after Vicki's findings. Both of them had their own questions to deal with and neither knew how to ask the other for the answers. Vicki wanted to know why Tildy looked so worried; almost afraid. She had never known her friend to be afraid of anything or anyone. Tildy wanted to know where Lady Jay had disappeared for so long. Why was she with Caring and what was she doing to make Caring so unhappy? Why was Lady Jay using a different name? How did James fit into this puzzle?

Chapter 4
James
The Good Son

James loved his mother without any doubt. Anybody who sat across from them would be able to tell that in a matter of minutes. He absolutely adored Lady Lorna J. She was extremely intelligent, beautiful, and successful. She was strong too. James knew that she had sacrificed being with him as a stay-at-home mom as she had always dreamed. After the sudden death of his father, she had to pick up the ministry his father had started. His mother had spent the majority of his childhood traveling all across the world spreading the Good News of Jesus Christ to all nations. She carried his father's legacy so that she could place it into his hands one day. What was not to adore about this woman of God? Of course, she missed his first steps; potty training; first days of school, holidays, and his high school graduation, but his aunt who was also a sweet, yet, simple woman much like his new wife, took many pictures and home videos she saved for his mother. His mother never missed a birthday, and always brought the photo albums she had with all of the pictures Aunt Leigha took. His mother always spoke life into him every time she came home, and this inspired him to preach the Gospel like she and his father.

James was convinced his mother had made hard decisions for the sake of securing his future. She was the driving force behind his enrolling and graduating from Libertine Seminary. It was his mother who also helped him secure his teaching position at Libertine. The letters of recommendation she had sent to the school were immaculately written according to Professor Shaw who also gave James a letter of recommendation. James owed his mother so much, and this is why he was in his current position.

Carrington Rebekah Mitchell was not James' type. She was a sweet girl, but she was not attractive to James. She was physically attractive to most men, but to James, she was too curvy and too smart for her own good. His mother became almost obsessed with her from the moment she saw her when she visited James at the school once. She saw Carrington from across the campus and totally lost track of the conversation she was having with him. She looked as if she had seen a ghost.

James remembered that he startled her when he reached and touched her to regain her attention. It was almost as if she had forgotten he was there. She immediately began asking questions about Carrington. Who was she, and did he know where she was from? Then, she demanded that he get to know as much as possible about her. So, James did exactly as he was told. He began to show interest in this girl who had caught his mother's eye.

It certainly was not a genuine interest. He just wanted to find out what he could to satisfy his mother. He figured that would be easy enough to do as most of the women on campus took a liking to his kind. James simply watched and waited for the opportunity to speak with her. It happened only a few days after his mother had given him orders. Knowing how Professor Shaw kept up with some of his star pupils was exactly what James needed to step into Carrington's world. He did not have to push or pull, James simply waited on an invitation.

He was ready with a rehearsed excitement when Professor Shaw asked him if he would join him on a trip to hear Carrington speak at her local church. It was not surprising to James that Carrington was a minister. She was bull-headed but anointed with a manly power from what he had heard from some of his male counterparts at Libertine. She was not the type satisfied to dress pretty and support from the side-line. This was one of the reasons James was devastated when his mother told him to pursue her. He only pictured himself in the spotlight with a First Lady, not with his lady first.

James had his own plans. He would accept the legacy his mother had been grooming him for and become a prestigious and prosperous pastor like that of his father or better. He would travel the world carrying and preaching the Gospel of Jesus accompanied by his mother and the woman he truly loved.   His plans were shattered when his mother announced that she had broken things off with his girlfriend for him so that he could openly pursue and woo Carrington.   James   was   absolutely flabbergasted by this because it seemed as if Lorna adored Tiffany.   What was even more astounding is that she told Tiffany over the phone that she and James needed to go their separate ways as he prepared for the Lord to move him higher. Tiffany called him at least fifty times, but his mother had already given him a new cell phone with a new number. James could not imagine what Tiffany must have thought of him when his mother told her the news.   He went days without sleeping until he finally told his mother that if Tiffany was not in the plan he knew she was devising, then he would not be able to do his part. His mind was not focused knowing that Tiffany was not in his life.   Lorna gave in to his one request, but after explaining to Tiffany that she had a plan that would assure that James would have a picture-perfect life that would afford   their   family   many   opportunities, Tiffany declined the invitation.   She never reached out to James again. James overheard the love of his life explain to his mother that she would not take any part in a mother-imposed scheme of wickedness. She made it clear that when James was able to discern truth, then, and only then, would he begin to walk as God had called him to do. It had been at least 6 years since he had heard from her, but time had not stopped him from loving her. Loving her had not stopped him from being obedient to his mother even though he knew what his mom was doing was wrong even if her motive was to give a secure future. Somehow, as she had always been able to do, she convinced James that this was fair and what she had been led to do.

James trusted her. His mom was his world even though he had begun to wonder about her mental stability. He knew she was taking medication, but every time he tried to engage her in a conversation about it, she shut him down harshly. Some things, she had made clear, were her business and only her business. Because he did not know how good or bad her health was, he just tried to keep her happy. If using Carrington was going to make her happy, Carrington would be sacrificed. After all, his own happiness had already been sacrificed. The thought of Tiffany with someone else was killing him slowly.

James remembered when he first met Tiffany. He and his cousin, Silas, were at The Pad shooting basketball. The Pad was where the neighborhood kids hung out picking up games and just enjoying a little freedom. Silas was his Aunt Lydia's youngest out of three. He and James were only a year apart. They were not enemies, but they were not friends. Silas and James tolerated one another. They competed against each other in everything; academics, sports, and girls. They kept things cordial after tiring from the beatings Uncle Jacob put on them when they were mere toddlers. Fighting was absolutely off-limits in his house. When they started school, Uncle Jacob became creative. He told them they could fight, but they would only fight his way or no way. Eager for the chance to demolish one another, they took the bait. Uncle Jacob signed them up for boxing lessons so they fought in the ring. He signed them up for karate classes so they competed on the mat. He signed them up for football, basketball, track, soccer, and baseball so they fought on the field and on the court. He demanded honor roll grades so they fought in the classroom. Uncle Jacob was fighting to make them men.

Silas and James were playing another intense game of one-on-one. Neither of them even saw the tall, thin girl enter The Pad and sit on the bleachers. Once again, they had lost themselves in the sport of competition. Both boys had sweat pouring off their faces as if someone had turned a hose on them, but neither would dare be the first to call the game; it was tied. Someone had to win, and someone had to lose.

"Make your move, man!" yelled Silas.

"Why are you in such a hurry to lose, Si?" James responded sarcastically. He knew how to get under Silas's skin, and enjoyed doing it.

"Do you ladies always carry on in such a way? I mean, come on, it's just a game."

James had barely turned his head in the girl's direction when Silas snatched the ball from his fingers and laid it up at the basket.

"YE-AH!!!!! GAME, Homeboy!!!!" Silas was celebrating his win so hard that he didn't notice that James could have cared less. Usually, James would still be talking smack and making some sort of excuse as to why Silas won, but not this time. Something else, or rather someone else, had his attention.

Silas walked over to grab their bags and towels from the side of the court. When he finally turned around, he saw James posted up on one knee looking into the face of some little girl. She was a thin little thing, Silas could tell even with her sitting down, and looked to be around their age. Whatever she was saying, James was doing a stellar job pretending he was interested. Silas thought she would soon find out that James was only interested in James. She wasn't really Silas's type, but he wanted to show his little cousin that he could push buttons too.

Silas walked over to the bleachers they occupied and took a seat right below the girl. He knew they had been sweating up a storm, so he dared not get too close, but sat just close enough to get her attention. He leaned back on the bleacher she was sitting on and looked up in her face until she looked down. She stared him right in his eyes.

"I know your mother taught you that it is impolite to stare, so mind your manners." She rolled her eyes and continued to talk to James about the classes she was taking.

"I know your daddy taught you to be respectful when you talking to a grown man." Silas waited until she looked in his direction, and then mocking her, rolled his eyes, and spoke to James.

"Man, when you get through flexing, let's go. I'm starving, and you know Dad will trip if we are late to dinner again."

"Silas, do you have to be rude all the time? Go ahead; I'll catch up with you."

Even though James spoke to Silas, he couldn't take his eyes off of Tiffany.

"NO! You know my mama will not let anybody eat until we are all at the table. LET'S GO!" His mother was sweet, but she had rules of her own that would not be ignored.

"Tiffany, I apologize for my cousin's ghetto behavior. His mother has taught him better, but fools despise correction. May I have your number?" James did not want to lose his cool in front of this angel. "I was hoping we could finish our conversation later."

"Look, Ms. Tiffany. If you want to start walking with us, be my guest. You look like you could use a meal that will stick to your bones." Silas laughed at his own joke and didn't even see James's fist flying toward his mouth.

His head rocked back, and he stumbled a little. "Have you lost your mind?" He yelled as he dropped the bag he had picked up and lunged towards James.

Weighing just a few pounds less than Silas, but being able to hold his own, James met Silas halfway. The two tussled with one another until Silas broke free and jabbed James in the eye. Tiffany began to yell for the two to stop fighting, but she had no idea that this fight was yet another competition. Not knowing who to get for help or what else to do, Tiffany picked up the basketball Silas had been playing with and started to beat both of them with it. She hit whomever wherever she could. Getting their attention, she yelled hysterically at both of them.

"I don't know who either of you has me confused with, but let's get this straight right now! I don't care what you think of me *or* my size! YOU don't know me, and I don't LIKE you!" she said to Silas. "And you. I won't deal with anybody that can't handle himself when someone is obviously trying to rattle his cage. YOU are going to have to come stronger and smarter than that if you want to get to know me!" With that said she threw the basketball down and began to walk home.

James looked at Silas with a look of disdain and ran to catch up with Tiffany. He liked her. He was not going to let her leave without giving him her number. He heard her and wanted her to know it. Silas snatched up his belongings, spit towards James's things, and started to walk home alone. He just wanted James to know he could rock his boat if he wanted and whenever he chose too.

After that day, James spoke to Tiffany every day before, during, and after school. They dated throughout high school and after they graduated. They were in love, and he was still in love, but now, he didn't know what was going to happen. He never thought this secret vendetta his mother had would go on for so long and get this far out of control. He did not even understand what it was all about.

Chapter 5
LADY LORNA J.
Manipulation Before Maturity

One might think that Lorna enjoyed making Carrington miserable. Actually Carrington was just a pawn in the game, and it was almost time to turn up the heat. Lorna thought that Carrington would have gone running home by now to tell mommy, but the girl proved to be stronger than she expected. Lorna did not hate Carrington; she hated where Carrington had come from and the reality she represented. It was her family that had ripped Lorna's fantasy to shreds. A fantasy that she had orchestrated from the moment she met J.C. No, she was not in love with him, but she loved what she had begun to groom him to be and the benefits she would reap from it.

J.C. was young when he first came to her father's church. He usually came with his alcoholic mama and sat in the back with her. It was obvious they didn't have anything. Most Sundays that he came his clothing was too small; his hair was wild; and his mama wore the same dress every time. His mother was the talk of the town. Not only was she known for her drinking, but she was also known for the brothel she called home and for fighting anybody that she deemed necessary to include her son. Even though he was only about ten, he stood tall and broad-shouldered. Her father took a special interest in him when J.C. walked to the front of the church, against his mother's will, and asked to be baptized. Lorna remembered the look on his mother's face and how she had stormed out of the church to never return. She didn't even come to J.C.'s baptism.

Lorna's father, Pastor Hubris Reaper, took J.C. under his wing. He personally taught J.C. everything he understood about the Holy Word. Lorna remembered not being allowed to tag along with him to the church because J.C. was being trained. This is what led to her envy of J.C. She was the apple of her daddy's eye even though she had an older sister. Her father made it obvious she was his favorite. Whatever Lorna wanted, Lorna would get. She knew that it was his way of buying her loyalty, but she could have cared less. Her mother often commented on how Leigha was more like her, and Lorna was definitely her father's child. The older she became, the more Lorna agreed with her mother's sentiment and was unapologetic about it.

Leigha *was* like their mother. She was weak and had their mother's passive attitude when situations arose that she did not know how to handle. Lydia, their mother, knew of her husband's infidelities but chose to turn a blind eye. The early morning meetings and late-night phone calls had kept Lydia in tears behind closed doors daily, but she always emerged looking put together and glowing with falsified happiness.

Leigha was her mother's daughter. She seemed to squirm every time their father entered the room. She shuttered when he spoke, and often cried when he reprimanded her. He never spanked her so Lorna didn't understand Leigha's fear. He only scolded her behind closed doors and never loud enough for anyone to hear. Leigha mainly got in trouble when their mother was away because she could never manage to get things done as their mother did. Lorna was different and determined to stay that way.

Lorna thought it was despicable and always vowed to never give a man such control. She decided she would start practicing on taking the upper hand with her father. She knew he was smart and powerful so she would have to be strategic and cautious; she needed to know his weakness. She soon discovered it by chance when she went to the church with him early one morning.

Lorna always dusted the sanctuary for her father every Saturday morning and put the hymnals out so they would be ready for the parishioners on Sunday morning. After she was done with her duties, she usually snuck to the kitchen to eat the communion crackers and sip just a little wine. One particular Saturday as she tiptoed past her father's study, she heard whimpering and low voices. She gently pressed her ear against the wooden door in an attempt to hear a little clearer. It sounded like it was Teeny Franklin from Leigha's Sunday school class. Was she saying "read" or "please"? Teeny was a hot tailed 13-year old that was being raised by her grandmother because her own mama didn't know what else to do with her. Not understanding why her father would be meeting with Teeny on Saturday morning baffled Lorna. Quietly turning the knob, she realized that the door was locked. This was even stranger. She had a weird feeling in the pit of her stomach. Lorna remembered what she had discovered the last time she unpicked a locked door and hesitated. Had her father a new mistress? Lorna had to get behind that door.

She walked just a few feet away from the door toward the kitchen. Then, as if she were being attacked by Satan himself, Lorna began to scream.

"DADDY!!! DADDY!!! DADDY, help me!!! HELP Me!!!" She jumped up and down like her feet were on fire. When she heard scuffling and bumping from behind the wall, Lorna turned toward her father's door and fell to the floor out of breath. Hubris came running out with his shirt unbuttoned and his belt unfastened, but where was Teeny?

"Baby Girl, what is it? Why are you on the ground?", he managed to huff out as he tried to gather himself. Lorna wondered why he was disheveled and out of breath.

"Where is Teeny?" she asked plainly. A look of confusion came over her father's face.

"What? How do you know Teeny is here?"

"She is too young a tramp for you, Daddy. Don't you see how she throws herself at J.C., and truth be told, he probably likes it. Where is she?" A sudden boldness had come over Lorna. She knew her hand was starting to come up.

"Look here, Young Lady. You will not use that terminology in the House of God nor will you question who, when, where, or how I counsel the lost. Do you understand me, Lorna? You are 12 years old, and you need to stay in your place." He looked convincing, but the nervousness in his voice gave him away.

"NO! I don't need to understand you, Daddy, but you need to understand that I won't let you control me like you do Mama and Leigha. You won't talk to me like you to talk to them either. So I won't question who, when, where, or how you handle the lost, but do I have question. What is counseling the lost worth to you?" A slow, deliberate smirk crossed her face.

"Now, Lorna, Baby Girl, you need to be careful. A lot of people can get hurt if you don't stay in your lane." She was met with her father's sly smile.

"RAPE!!!!!! RAPE!!!!! HELP US, PLEAAASSSEEE!!!!" she began to scream like a lunatic all over again.

Stunned at her performance, Hubris didn't realize the boy, now, standing beside him looking horrified.

"LORNA!!!! OKAY, Baby Girl, PLEASE stop before someone in the neighborhood calls the police!" Hubris was not only angry and terrified, but he was also shocked at how easily his own had turned on him. He thought he had all three of his girls under control.

Hubris was not the only one in shock. Lorna didn't stop her antics because he told her too. She had not realized that J.C. was in the study too. He must have come through the kitchen with Teeny after she and Daddy had arrived at the church.

"J.C.? What are you doing in there?! And why is that tramp in there with you and my daddy?!" Lorna stopped screaming but didn't try to lower her voice.

Teeny came limping from the study trying to hold her shirt closed and looked as if she had been crying. She looked at Lorna with a look of anguish and perplexity. Why was this little girl calling her a tramp? Was she completely unaware of her Father's sins? As Lorna questioned Hubris and J.C., Teeny took the opportunity to run up the hall into the sanctuary and out of the door. Lorna made a mental note to deal with her later.

"J.C., gather your things and go on home, Boy. I'll talk with you later." Like a lost puppy, he did exactly what he was told. With the two of them left alone, Hubris, defeated, attempted to manipulate his youngest daughter with a speech on loyalty.

"IF you want me to keep my mouth shut, why don't you just ask me, Daddy?" She smiled sweetly using his manipulative tactics on him.

Hubris realizing that his daughter had taken more than just his looks from him, succumbed to this new attitude he saw in her. Maybe it had always been there, and he was too self-centered to see it.

"Lorna, please, don't ever mention this to anyone. Will you do this for me?" He was begging. Pastor Hubris Reaper was begging. She won.

"Ok, Daddy, I won't." Lorna, then, straightened her dress, wiped her face, and turned to walk to the kitchen. She waited until she heard her Daddy's sigh of relief and the creak of his door. "But, Daddy?" she stopped and turned to look him in the face.

Hubris tiredly gave her his full attention. "Yes, Lorna?"

"It's definitely going to cost you." She turned and added a little bounce to her step as she hummed the hymn, "You Don't Know What the Lord Told Me".

Lorna remembered these things and so much more about her childhood that she wished she could forget. So many things happened that only she; her sister; and their parents knew about. With both of her parents gone now, only she and her sister were left with the detestable memories of dysfunction. Leigha had somehow made peace with it all. Even the memories that could not be erased; the memories that had living evidence which made them unforgettable and unforgivable in her eyes. Her sweet sister had made peace with it all. Perhaps one day she would have that sort of peace, but until then, she would continue to allow the voices in her head to advise her. They had been her only source of comfort for decades. They kept her from becoming weak and passive like her sister and mother. She would keep them around, at least, until her husband's death, or rather the death of her fallacy, was avenged. Then, she would stop pretending and truly do what she knew her sister was still praying for her to do.

Chapter 6
Carrington
Mama's Here

There was definite newness about Carrington. Perhaps it was the conversation she had with her mother just a little over a week ago. Maybe it was the meaning she took from the conversation, and the unfailing love she could feel as she finally heard what her mother was saying to her. She replayed their conversation over and over in her mind until she had it memorized. There was no doubt she would need the reminder of what was spoken in the time to come especially when Lady showed up. Carrington knew Lady was going to show, but this time she was going to meet someone she had not met before. Lady Lorna J. was about to be introduced to the real Carrington Rebekah MITCHELL Reaper. James had no clue that she had spoken to her mother, and Carrington decided to leave it that way for now. As she prepared dinner, she thought back to the three-hour conversation that was more needed than she thought when she decided to call home.

"Hello." One common word came from Tilda's mouth, and Carrington's tears begin to flood and fall from her eyes.

"Caring, I know this is you, Child." Tilda was never one to mix words or pacify a situation.

"Mama, I'm sorry." Carrington didn't know how her mother would respond to her sorrowful apology, but she knew an apology was necessary and did not know any other way to say it. She held her breath waiting on her mother's response.

"How are you, Caring?" It was so astonishing that her mother completely overlooked her apology. She immediately calmed herself and stopped crying.

"Mama, I'm so sorry. Please forgive me for being disobedient." Perhaps if she used a more direct approach and confessed to her defiance, her mother would be more responsive.

"Caring, if you only knew all the things that I knew, you would know that I love you and could never withhold my love and forgiveness from you."

What was going on? This was not at all how she thought the conversation would go. She was not expecting Tilda to be hateful, but she never expected for her to be this calm either.

"How are you, Caring? I really would like to know." Tilda sounded so undisturbed and concerned. Carrington could hear no signs of anger in her mother's voice at all, and she wanted to keep it that way so she decided to just follow Tilda's lead.

"Mama, to be honest, I am not happy." She tried to approach the situation like an adult and with honesty. "James is not cruel to me or anything. It's just that......he...."

"What is it, Caring? It's that he is just what?" Tilda remained relaxed.

"Mama, he's such a ...... a Mama's Boy!!! It's like this lady has him in a never-ending trance. Even when she is not here, she is still controlling his mind and decisions. He is NOT the man I fell in love with and who swept me off of my feet." Carrington had to make herself slow down. She did not want Tilda to come there and tear James's house down.

"Caring, calm down, Sweetheart. That does not sound like the end of the world. Is there something else going on that would have you distraught to tears? Can you talk about it?" Try as she might, Carrington knew she had to tell her mama everything.

"Mama, the worst part is that............." Carrington paused not knowing how her mother would respond.

"Yes, he's what, Honey. Tell me." Now she sounded anxious for Carrington to tell her; almost holding her breath as if she knew had a preconceived notion of what was coming next.

"Mama, he's celibate!!! I never suspected it as intensely flirtatious as he had been. He flat out refuses to be sexually intimate with me. Our kisses have watered down to pecks on the lips behind closed doors and pecks on the cheek when in the company of others." She already felt a sense of relief venting to her Mama. "Mama, we don't even share a bedroom. I'm so full of disappointment every time I see a couple with their children knowing that will never be James and me."

Carrington thought she heard Tilda sigh with relief. Why would such news relieve her mother when she knew how much Carrington loved James and wanted to start a family with him? Carrington had talked about having a family since she was a young child playing with dolls. She always felt like something was missing in her life because she never knew her own father. Carrington hoped that having her own child would fill that void.

"Caring, there is always disappointment, disaster, and sometimes danger in rushing into things without any understanding of what is before us. Sometimes we fool ourselves into thinking we are exercising our faith. We pride ourselves and make attempts to justify our behavior by taking the Scripture out of context. Faith is the substance of things hoped for and the evidence of things not seen. Faith belief in God to do that which you hope for even when you don't see how He's doing it and you don't know when it will come to past, but you know God is working things out on your behalf. You trust His plan. You trust He knows what you need and what you want. Faith is not running ahead of God and believing that He is going to follow your lead and approve your plans. You can do what you want with your free will, but understand if it is not of His Will and His Timing, no matter how good it begins, consequences will be faced before it's all said and done."

Tilda could hear Carrington's sniffles and knew her words were piercing her daughter's tender heart, but she knew the words had to be spoken. Carrington would have to face many things in the time to come, and only God's Word would strengthen and equip her to handle those things if she received it.

"Mama, I know you're upset about me leaving. I am truly sorry for running off and marrying James without your consent, but I don't need to hear an eloquent I-told-you-so speech right now. I need comfort and reassurance that everything is going to be alright. Mama, I do still love my husband."

Carrington knew her mother was not built this way, but she needed what she needed. She was aware that she was wrong in how she went about this entire situation. This was the reaping of the deceit and rebellion she had sown; however, she needed to hear that everything was going to soon be resolved. Her mother was right in everything she spoke, but Carrington just couldn't deal with what she knew to be the truth at this moment.

"Child of God, Daughter of my womb, everything is going to be alright; you are equipped with a strong foundation and enduring faith. Hold on, Child. Hold on." Tilda did not waiver from her firm tone, but she spoke to what her daughter desperately requested.

It was true. Everything was going to be alright, but Tilda also knew that sometimes things have to be broken and destroyed before they are built back up better and stronger. One has to face their ignorance to gain a better understanding. Carrington needed to hold on and hold on tight because life was about to take a twist, flip, and knock her down. She needed to get a good grip of God's hand if she was to endure the faith-testing blow. It was Tilda's desire to help her daughter as much as she could during this test and trial, but Carrington was in The Potter's hands. Tilda wanted to know more about this man Carrington defied her for and the woman whom Vicki thought was Lady Jay.

"Caring, I know my strong distrust of James perhaps drove your infatuation with him. Maybe I did not give him a fair chance because he reminded me so much of someone from my past in the way he carries himself. Tell me more about your husband."

"Mama, he isn't a bad person. He really does love ministering and teaching the Word of God. He is not cruel to me but treats me more like the help than his wife unless we are in the company of others. When we are alone, he treats me like a good buddy, but it is nowhere near like it was before we were married." Carrington had almost slipped back down memory lane when her mother's voice interrupted her thoughts.

"What changed, Caring? Why would a man go through the trouble of battling your parents and whisk you off in the night to wed you to only become friends? Do you think there may be someone else? Maybe you were an attempt to make someone else notice him? I'm only asking." Tilda knew James didn't love Caring. Caring was not at all his speed. There had to be a reason behind his determination to take Caring away.

"Oh, no, Mama. James would not dare tarnish his reputation with that type of pettiness. The only other woman in this relationship is Lady Lorna J. He has made it painfully clear that I am no competition for her."

"Lady Lorna J.?"

"HIS mother. Mama, she's so arrogant and domineering. James does whatever she tells him to do. She acts as if she is his wife, and I'm the maid."

"She treats you like the help? Where is she from?" Tilda was trying to change the subject. The thought of someone mistreating her only child made her blood boil.

"Yes, I don't think she likes me at all, and I have no idea why. I believe I heard James mention she grew up in Bay City, Michigan."

Tilda was even more curious about her now. Pastor Hewman was from the Bay City area too.

"Caring, does his father ever visit?"

"No, apparently he died before James was born, but James attempts to live up to what he believes would be his father's expectations. It's apparent Lady Lorna raised him to idolize his father."

Oh, no, please! NO! Tilda thought she was going to be sick. There were too many pieces to this puzzle all coming together at once. His parents were from Michigan. His father died before he was born. His mother's cruel demeanor toward Carrington for no apparent reason. These were not coincidences. Tilda didn't believe in coincidences. She wanted to warn Carrington, but she had no solid evidence. Tilda knew Carrington would never just leave her husband because of her motherly intuition that something was off about her mother-in-law. She knew she had to see this woman for herself.

"Caring?"

"Yes, Mama."

"Caring, it's so good to hear your voice even though you're not as happy as I hoped you would be."

"Mama, you don't know how badly I've wanted to call you especially when Monster Dearest is in town. I hate feeling so alone in my home."

"Would you like some company, Honey?"

"Mama, *you* would come here to *visit*? After everything James and I have done?"

"Carrington Rebekah Mitchell, you are still my child. Would you like me to come for a visit?"

"Yes, Yes, YES!!!"

"When would be a good time? I would love to meet your *delightful* Monster-In-Law." Tilda gave a forced chuckle to hide her anger.

"Two weeks from now, she's coming back. She usually comes once or twice a month, but Mama, let me prepare James. No disrespect, but I need some time."

"Well, Love, I look forward to it whenever you're ready. Are you okay? Financially?"

"Yes, Mama, I'm fine. I can't wait to see you, but Mama, please don't say anything to my husband about what we have discussed." Carrington was angry at James, but she still loved him. He was still her husband, and she would not have him embarrassed about anything that she had disclosed to her mother.

"I won't, Caring. All we discuss is between the two of us. I better go. I will discuss this little trip with your Pop. I love you, Caring, please know this and nothing can change that." Tilda hung up first.

Carrington felt a huge weight lifted from her shoulders. It felt good to confess to her mother. To ask for and receive her mother's forgiveness was a blessing, and one she did not take for granted. She couldn't wait to see her mother and to wrap her arms around her. Carrington decided not to even tell James about her mother's visit because she knew he would find a reason to delay it; however, she had to admit she was nervous about the mothers meeting.

Chapter 7

James
Alone In the Dark

"James! Hi, Baby. What brings you back this way?" Leigha always met all with a sweet humble demeanor. She made even the toughest of the tough soften when she smiled. James loved her because she had always been there.

James didn't know how or where to begin. He felt like he was betraying his mother. Neither she nor Carrington knew he had come into the city to see his aunt. His mother had specifically told him not to tell her sister of her visits with him. When James had inquired why it had to be such a secret, she lashed out at him about how disrespectful it was for him to side with her sister instead of obeying her. She told James how his aunt was always in her business and jealous of her because she was their father's favorite and had been allowed to travel the world. His mother made it clear she did not want her sister in her business now that he was an adult or continuing to try and raise James as her own. Even though James could not imagine his dear aunt behaving in such a manner, he didn't want his mother to even suspect that he loved his Aunt Leigha more than he loved her. It wasn't until he noticed his mother's strange behavior and outburst that he became worried. He needed to talk to somebody. James needed someone to help him sort things out, and he knew Aunt Leigha could do it.

"Aunt Leigha, I'm worried about my mother. She's different." James was nervous about this entire conversation.

He did not want to hear anyone's negative judgment of his mother, but he knew Aunt Leigha knew his mother better than anyone else. If anyone could figure out what was going on with his mother, it was Aunt Leigha. Leigha turned from putting away her groceries to look at her nephew. She had a strange look on her face as if she were confused about what James was talking about.

"James, when have you seen your mother?" James had never been to the hospital to visit his mother. Lorna had always made it clear to Leigha that James was to never visit her at, what she called, 'The Facility'. "Honey, how did you know where to find my sister?"

"What do you mean how did I find her? She flew in to see me rather than meet me here. She's been visiting me at Libertine since my freshmen year of college. Why are you looking at me like that?" James didn't understand her questions or her confusion. "Aunt Leigha, I don't understand."

"Oh my, God, please be gracious and merciful." Leigha dropped down in the nearest chair of her breakfast table. "James, what do you mean different? I haven't seen or heard from my sister since your second semester at Libertine. Please, tell me what's going on with Lorna?"

Now, James just saw worry and fear on his aunt's sweet face. She twisted her fingers together as if she were just as nervous as he was when he first entered her home.

James suddenly knew if his aunt was this disturbed by his news, she had good reason to be. Leigha was not a high strung person so something was definitely wrong.

"Aunt Leigha, she has outburst. She becomes so enraged so easily when she's having a bad day. I mean when she's feeling well, she has such energy! She's happy, laughing, and talking a mile a minute. I can barely keep up with her, but...." James stopped in mid-thought. He had not thought about it until he was speaking out loud about his mother. His mother was her normal self until Carrington was around. She was fine until the weekend came to an end, and James left her in Carrington's care. The longer she stayed around Carrington the more irritated and angry she became. Carrington seemed to agitate his mother's fragile state of mind.

"James? But what, Honey?" Leigha knew what James was going to say, but she wanted him to say it so that she would not have too.

"I wasn't really concerned at first, but she has started to have more bad days than good. Bad days usually followed after a night of bad dreams, and she would take her medicine and rest during the next day. By the time I would return home from my assignments, she would be back to her normal self. After, I met Carrington; her bad days became more frequent. It's like Carrington is her..."

"Trigger?" Leigha couldn't help but finish his statement. "James, who is Carrington? Why haven't you brought her to see us? You hardly even talk about her at all."

"Aunt Leigha, I didn't come to talk about my wife. I came because something is wrong with my mother, and I need your help to figure out what it is and how to help. Please, let's stay focused." James didn't mean to be so blunt with her, but he was anxious to help his mother.

"First of all, you will not walk into my home and speak to me like I am slow. Secondly, I don't need to figure out what is wrong with my sister because I already know. The only thing I need to do is figure out what she has told you, and how to help you digest secrets that must be exposed. Now, tell me who this Carrington is from Alabama?"

James was shocked by the sternness in his aunt's voice. "Aunt Leigha, I'm terribly sorry. I just don't know what's going on, and I'm worried." James did not want to turn away the only help he knew he could count on. "Carrington is the daughter of Tilda Larain Mitchell from a small town in Alabama. Her mother is a minister and has been since she was eleven years old so goes the story. She fell by the wayside for years, but eventually gave herself back to the Lord and is pastoring and expanding the church my father pastored before his death."

"Leigha, it's time to tell the truth." Both, James and Leigha looked toward the entrance to the kitchen where his uncle Jacob stood. "All of it." Jacob turned and walked toward the formal living room.

Without looking at James, Leigha followed her husband. James didn't know what he was about to find out, but he knew it would reveal things about his mother that would help him help her. He could not help but ponder what it was going to do to his own mental health.

"Son, first let me say that everything your aunt and I have done has been to protect you and make sure your mother received the help she desperately needs." Jacob chose his words carefully.

"Pops? Mom? We're here! Where are you?" Silas walked into the room and was surprised to see his cousin. "James? To what do we owe the honor of having you bestow your affluent presence in our humble dwelling?" Silas' words were dripping with sarcasm.

"Si, don't start!" Just as quickly as Silas started, his father had ended it.

"Hey, Pop and Ma. Oh, my!" Tiffany couldn't believe her eyes. She had not spoken to James in years. Now, she was looking into his face.

"Tiffany?" James felt his heartbeat speeding up. She was still as beautiful as he remembered. "What are you doing here?"

Silas moved to her side and placed his arms around her waist. "She's my wife, Cousin." Silas planted a gentle kiss on the top of his wife's head.

He couldn't believe what he had just heard. Did Silas really just call Tiffany his wife? How could they do this to him? He knew he needed to finish this conversation with his aunt and uncle, but not now. He felt like the room was closing in around him; he had to get out.

"Uncle Jacob, Aunt Leigha, I have to go." James snatched up the jacket that he had thrown over the arm of the chair he was sitting in before Silas and Tiffany had entered and interrupted his world. He pushed past Silas and bumped his shoulder as he headed towards the front door.

"Watch it, Cousin!" Silas yelled toward James's back.

"Son, please, just a minute! We really need to talk to you!" Jacob pleaded, but it was too late. They heard the front door slam and the roar of an engine. James screeched out of their driveway.

James didn't realize how fast he was going until he saw the two police cars ahead of him. He slowed his speed, but his mind kept racing. He couldn't believe Silas and Tiffany were married! How could Tiffany have stooped this low as to marry his blood? No one said it, but she looked pregnant too! The more he thought about it the more infuriated he became. Sitting at the stop light right before his hotel, James begin slamming his fist into the empty passenger seat beside him. He knew that eventually she might move on, but with Silas? It had to be about revenge. As he rubbed his aching fist, and turned into the hotel parking garage, he begin to think about his aunt and uncle.

He knew he couldn't go home in the state of mind that he was currently in, so James went right to the customer service desk and paid for another night. He had come to find answers and only seemed to have more questions. His mother knew him like the back of her own hand, or at least how he felt for her, so he knew she would drill him until he caved if he went home while she was there. Once he made it to the serenity of his hotel suite, he sat down to call home.

"Hello, Reaper Residence." He had never paid attention to the calm smooth tone of Carrington's voice before. Her "hello" made his racing heart slow down. "Hello?"

"Oh, Carrington, I, um, I didn't hear you pick up. Where is Mother?" James was surprised at his own hesitation with Carrington. He had to recover quickly before Carrington suspected something was wrong.

"James, your mother is in her room resting I assume. We need to discuss some things I've noticed going on with her." James didn't know that Carrington had really noticed the changes with his mother. "It has gone far beyond her calling you by your father's name. What time will you be in tonight?" She sounded very concerned about her in spite of how terrible his mother had made a habit out of treating her. Still, James didn't want to discuss his mother with Carrington at this point. He needed more answers first.

"Carrington, I don't have time to discuss these things you're seeing with you yet. Please, put my mother on the phone, now." For the first time, James felt awful about how he was speaking to her, but it had to be this way for the time being. He could not take the risk of becoming weak and distracted until he knew what was happening to his mother.

"Fine, James. I understand that you do not care to consider my concerns when it comes to mother, but please talk with someone. I think she may be a danger to herself."

James felt like someone had pricked his heart. He felt like an animal that had just pounced on his prey. He figured he had to be emotional because he had just witnessed the love of his life with his cousin. What was happening to him? When would his life go back to normal?

"Carrington, put – my – mother – on - the telephone. NOW!" He was becoming angrier even though none of his anger was because of Carrington. It had just become so easy to lash out at her, but James knew he was wrong. "Carrington, I'm sorry. I should not have yelled at you like that." It was a very poor attempt at an apology.

"James? James, is this you, son?" His mother didn't sound like herself at all. "She keeps following me and watching me from around corners, James. When are you coming home? Had I known you were going to be out of town for so long, I would have stayed home."

"Mother, who keeps following and watching you? Carrington?" James was even more concerned now. His mother's mental health was in serious trouble.

"James, just come home. I leave tomorrow, and we need to talk about the next part of the plan." Now, she was whispering.

"Mother, I'm sure Carrington is not following you. She's just making sure that you want for nothing while I am away. She knows how important you are to me." As the words were coming from his mouth, James thought about how kind and considerate

Carrington was towards his mother no matter how much his mother verbally abused her. "Mother, perhaps you could take it easy with the insults. Carrington just wants to please you." James was sure that the only reason a woman would take this much abuse from her mother –in-law is because of the love she has for that mother's son. "Besides, this is why you really should call me before you come for a visit." James held his breath for his mother's angry outburst.

"Good-bye, James. I will start the next phase of the plan and fill you in later." Click. James couldn't believe she hung up on him.

What did she mean by next part of the plan? As much as he hated the thought of it, he knew he had to go back to his aunt and uncle. They had the answers he needed. He laid back on the bed in the dark. He had never felt this alone before. The people who raised him had secrets they felt the need to come clean about. His mother, his idol, seemed to be falling apart as she sought revenge on an enemy he didn't even really know for reasons he didn't understand. The love of his life no longer belonged to him even if she did only belong to him in his heart; she now belonged to his first cousin. The only person left was the person he treated the worse: Carrington. Perhaps, now, she would listen to him, and try to help him find help for his mother had he treated her better after they were married. He had to tell her as much of the truth as he knew. Their whole meeting; fantasy courting; and fairytale wedding was a setup he took part in to satisfy his mother. This would devastate her. He was alone and felt the darkness suffocating him. James knew there was only one thing to do; something he had not done in a while now. There was someone else to turn too.

He slid off of the bed to the floor. He landed on his knees with his arms outstretched, and he began to cry out. James was not concerned with anyone hearing him. He cried like a lost lamb. When he was able to take in air between his sobs, he began to call on the name of Jesus. Before he could even think about hearing out his aunt and facing Carrington, He needed to talk to the only One who could help him endure the reaping of his sins. His Aunt Leigha used to always tell them, that when you couldn't form the words in your mind for your mouth to speak there was but one name you needed to get out: JESUS.

"Jesus. Jesus. JESUS!!! I am so messed up!" When the words begin to come, James couldn't stop them. They rolled off of his tongue as easy as the tears rolled down his face.

"JESUS!!! I am lost. I am hurt. I am confused, and I am in the midst of hurting someone that deserves so much better. My Lord and Savior, forgive me, and clean me up. Wash me and make me whole again. Create in your wayward son a clean heart, and renew a right spirit within me. I am weak, but You, Father, are mighty. Give me your strength to stand up for right and be the man you would have me to be. I love my mother, but I place her in Your hands. I love my uncle and aunt; help me to love them after truths are revealed. Help Tiffany to forgive me for the pain I caused her by being a weak immature man, and help me to forgive her and Silas for being together and finding true love. Father, you said he who finds a wife, finds a good thing and obtains favor with you. IF Carrington is not my wife, strengthen me to let her go. Guide her to her husband so that she is given love as genuinely as she gives it, and she is loved as hard as she loves others. IF she is to remain with me, my rib and my helpmeet, teach me to love this princess of Your Kingdom as You love the church. Help me to be the provider; the friend; the lover it is in Your will for such a daughter to have and in a way that glorifies you. Let her heart be softened toward me that she will forgive my iniquities and receive this love. I want to love my wife in a way that drives her closer to you; she can't help but exalt you when she thinks about us. I don't want to be the man I am any more. I don't want to be the man my *mother* planned for me to be. I want to be a true God-fearing man. I want to be the man *You* created me in my mother's womb to be. Abba, let *Your* will be done." He continued to just lay there on the floor, face down, and in total submission to the Lord. By the time his tears stopped flowing, James had fallen into a deep sleep.

Chapter 8
Carrington
Suffering Sophistication

Carrington didn't know how she was going to approach this situation with James. For two days, he had been gone to Atlanta, Georgia, to some conference that just happened to be on the same weekend that his mother had decided to visit. He swore he tried to get out of it, but couldn't find anyone to go in his place at such short notice. He even blamed his mother for popping in on him without notice. Carrington thought he was the one that was delirious being she always popped in and out as she pleased, so why was he suddenly frustrated? She was the one who should have been frustrated being that she would be left alone to chauffeur, cook, clean, and be at the beck and call of Lady Lorna all weekend. What made the situation even worse was that Carrington did not believe for one second that James was going to a conference especially now since he had changed his plans so he could stay another night!

Truth of the matter was James had been spending a lot of time away from home, especially when his mother was in town. It was as if he was not only doing his usual to avoid Carrington, but now, he seemed to be avoiding his own mother too. Carrington had learned from her mother that the only thing that could keep a man away from the woman who birthed him was anger toward his mama or the love of another woman, and James never got angry with Lady Lorna. She figured he had met someone at Libertine, as he did her, and was having an affair. Even though they were not physically intimate, the thought of James with someone else upset Carrington. Thoughts of him confiding in and laughing with someone else, infuriated her. That is, after all, what he *used* to do with her or was it *all* just a game? She didn't know him and perhaps, she never did really know him. She had not seen the man she fell so in love with in a very long time.

Lady Lorna was bothered by his behavior too, but he was never home long enough for her to express her dissatisfaction. Carrington knew Lady Lorna hated not having her usual audience to listen and watch her tortuous behavior. She was still hateful to Carrington and seemed to take her anger for James out on her when he was away. Her ill treatment still did not camouflage her strange behavior.

Carrington noticed only little changes at first, such as, calling James "J.C.". Lady Lorna would attempt to laugh it off with the excuse that James reminded her of him more and more. Then, there was the time that Lady Lorna seemed almost afraid of her. She seemed to be accusing Carrington of something, but she had a weird glazed look in her eyes.

It started off like any other morning. Lady Lorna came down stairs and entered the family room and sat in the oversized recliner she claimed as her own. She begin to work on her crossword puzzles and pretended like Carrington was thin air.

"Good Morning, Lady Lorna, I'll go and prepare breakfast. Eggs and toast or would you prefer Apple Cinnamon Oatmeal?" Carrington was so tired of this foolishness. She put her devotional Bible on the end table, and headed toward the kitchen, but stopped short of leaving the room when she noticed there was no response. "Lady Lorna? I didn't hear your preference."

Lady Lorna's eyes never left her puzzle book. This was just outlandishly disrespectful. "LORNA!" It came out a lot louder and harsher than Carrington had intended it.

Lady Lorna looked up at Carrington with a puzzled look in her eyes. "How did you get in here? Get away from me!!! I saw you! I know what you did, and you will pay!!" She jumped up, letting her book fall to the floor. Carrington backed up bracing herself for an attack, but Lady Lorna ran past her and up the stairs as if she were being pursued by a murderous maniac. Carrington couldn't even put into words what had just happened, but she knew she had to tell James.

After several incidences of the same, Carrington was still trying to figure out how to tell James that his mother was losing her mind.   It was as if, Lorna was stuck somewhere in time.   Things were escalating though. It seemed after every episode, hours later, Lady Lorna would float down stairs and act as if nothing had ever happened. This was not normal, and she knew something needed to be said and done.

Lady Lorna seemed to live in a world that no one else could visibly see. If she wasn't trying to escape from Carrington's presence, she was accusing Carrington of following her; watching her; and even stealing from her.   She kept telling Carrington that she was going to get back what was taken from her.   Carrington tried to find out what she had taken from Lady Lorna, but this only seemed to make matters worse so she tried to stay out of her way.   She dared not get to far away from Lady Lorna for fear that she would burn down the house or wonder too far off of the property during one of her hallucinations.

Carrington had found half completed crossword puzzles all over the house. Coffee cups were all over the place because after forgetting where she sat one cup, Lady would simply go fix another cup. When Carrington would gently confront her, Lady would act as if she had no idea what Carrington was talking about. What really bothered Carrington, even more so than the accusations, were the voices that Lady swears she heard. Voices that were either speaking about her; to hear; or keeping secrets that she felt she deserved to know. Carrington asked her on several occasions if she recognized the voices, but Lady would just stare at her and refuse to answer.

One day Carrington saw Lady standing with her ear to the door of one of the other guest rooms. Putting the basket of laundry down, she asked Lady if there was something she needed from the room.

"Sh-h-h-h-h-h-h-h." Lady Lorna placed her index finger to her mouth in an effort to quiet Carrington. She motioned for her to meet her in the middle of the hallway. Carrington decided to entertain her.

"What is it?" she whispered, "Is someone in there?"

"They're in there again. I told her Daddy didn't want her talking to that boy Jacob. Daddy got so mad when he seen that slick boy carrying her books from school. I thought he was going to yank her arm off when she came in the house. Oh, well, if she would just do what he wanted, Daddy wouldn't get on to her so much." Lady Lorna suddenly looked down the stairs toward the front door as if she heard something. When Carrington turned from her in an attempt to see what she was looking for, Lady turned away and went to her room. Without another word, she shut her door.

Who did she hear behind the closed door? Why was she speaking in that tone? Her voice almost sounded like a teenage girl instead her usual stuffy sophisticated and articulate dialect. She sounded so convincing that against her better judgment, Carrington went to the guest room door and put her ear to it. Thinking about how ridiculous she looked, she stood up and turned the knob. As she entered the room, she thought how none of this made sense.

The room was empty like she knew it would be, and everything was in its place.

There were more occurrences of voices. Carrington couldn't get Lady to provide names to go with any of them, but she definitely knew one that was reoccurring: Lady Lorna's father.

Chapter 9

James

Old Things Have Passed Away

Things had been different since James returned home from his "Atlanta conference". Carrington made sure to stay out of his way as she always did, but he hoped that she could see there was something different about him. She had once told him that she liked to collect bells from different places she had traveled. To her surprise, he brought her back a bell from Atlanta with a peach orchard drawn on it. He could tell she was more surprised by his excitement to give it to her than she was to receive it. She thanked him, and he gently kissed her cheek and thanked her for caring for his mother while he was away. He walked away while she stood there with her mouth gaped open. He wondered how she was going to react to his next surprise for her.

Most mornings he was gone before she awakened, and in the evenings, he ate dinner in his study. Now, he ate dinner in the dining room and breakfast in the kitchen with her. When he returned from Atlanta, the first thing he did was convince his mother that work was going to have him pretty tied up so it was best that she go on home. Besides, Christmas was just a couple of months away so it would not be too long before she was on her way back. He called her housekeeper, Erin, to make sure she made it to the train station to pick her up before the train arrived so Lady was not kept waiting. He was so much more relaxed when he returned from seeing her off.

There was a light tap on Carrington's door about two nights after Lady Lorna had been sent home by her devoted son. Carrington was already dressed for bed and was sitting in her reading nook writing in her journal. She had no idea why James would be visiting her room at this hour. With his mother already gone, there was no one for her to get a glass of water for or bring extra pillows too. He knew she would be suspicious about his visit. Her curiosity must have gotten the best of her because she finally answered.

"Yes, James?" Slowly inching the door open, James popped his head inside. It was almost enough to make Carrington chuckle. "Is something wrong?"

"Carrington, may I come in? I'm sorry I waited so late; I see you're dressed for bed. I can't sleep." James looked almost sad.

This further peaked Carrington's curiosity. Something was definitely bothering him, but he wanted to proceed with caution. He had prayed that God would give him the right words to say to her, but this was not going to be as easy as he hoped. James mostly prayed that she would be open to talk with him; though, he had truly been cruel to her.

"Give me a few minutes. We can have some coffee in the family room. IF you like?" James wondered if she was trying not to sound as anxious as he did.

"I'll go make the coffee, and see you in a few minutes. Take your time." He started to close the door again, but suddenly reappeared. "Carrington?"

"Yes?" She turned as she put away her journal and reached for her robe.

"Thank you." Then, he was gone.

If she had not been awake already, she would have said this was only a dream. She was wide awake, and this was not a dream. God was up to something, and this was only the beginning.

James decided to set a comfortable atmosphere with hopes to relax Carrington. He put one of the records he knew she liked on the antique record player. As soon as the thread touched the vinyl the smooth sounds of light jazz filled the family room. It made James look around the room and take notice. What good is a family room without family? When he came back from his thoughts, Carrington was seated in the love seat across from the sofa.

During the time he was actively seducing her for his mother's gain, James learned how Carrington liked her coffee. He

135

stopped making it for her after he had her trapped so he was not surprised or offended when she hesitated to take the coffee mug from his hands.

"It's okay, Carrington. I just want to talk." James purposely touched her hand as she reached for the cup. "I assure you this is not a game."

He had not taking the time to look into Carrington's eyes for a long time. He saw confusion and sadness. What had he allowed himself to be talked into by his mother? How was he going to come out of this, and why would God even help him after what he had done. It was time to end this. He watched her as she cautiously sipped her coffee. Realizing that she was not going to relax in his presence anytime soon, he decided to start talking.

"Carrington, I need to tell you something. I know it's going to hurt you, and if you choose to leave I won't try to stop you." Fearfully, James lifted his head and met her eyes. She had not moved, and they had not changed. She didn't make a sound.

"I knew who you were when I came to Holy Ghost Fulfillment Baptist Church. I mean.....I knew about you. I knew of your mother too." James waited to see if she would respond. She still said nothing.

"My mother saw you on campus one day, and demanded that I pursue you. When I continued to argue and ask questions about her deal with you, she said I just needed to do what she was asking for the sake of our family. I know I should have asked more, but I didn't. I agreed to seduce you and marry you when I....I .....Carrington" James hesitated.

"You were not interested, and you didn't love me." She cut him off with the words he couldn't even say anymore. He wondered if the words tasted as disgusting to her as they did in his own mouth. "It took a while, but I figured it out, James." She took another sip of her coffee.

"When? Why didn't you say anything? It doesn't matter." He dropped his head and stared into his coffee cup. "I am dead wrong, and I am so sorry, Carrington. I intentionally hurt you, and there are no excuses." He didn't know what else to say.

"You're right; it doesn't matter now. Now, I am your wife, and you are my husband. We are married, James. The question, I guess, is where we go from here." Why was she so calm about his confession? He would have hit the roof after being told he had been set up for unknown reasons.

"I don't know, Carrington. I never wanted to get married to get divorced. There is something else you need to know."

Confessing about his own dirt was one thing, but discussing his mother's fragile state was another. He knew the contempt Carrington held in concerning his mother, but he didn't know what he would say or do if she let it out in this moment. He had to tell her, now, because he needed to know what she had noticed about his mother's recent behavior.

"Something is going on with my mother. She hasn't been herself in the last few months, and I am kind of worried about her mental health. I always suspected some mental instability, but something is really wrong now. What have you noticed, Carrington?"

"So this is why you've been so different since coming from Atlanta? Is this why you're being so kind to me? James saw something else in her eyes; anger. "You're worrying about your mother, and you need to know if I know anything. WOW!"

"All this time, I thought you were having an affair, but nope, that would be too easy and unbecoming of the dignified-always- all-together- James Caleb Reaper so maybe you are celibate. No, you were baiting me, once again, to get what you wanted." He did not know Carrington even possessed this type of temper. "You just confessed to bringing me here so she could torture me as she chooses! Now, that she's the one who's breaking, you want me to help you figure out what's wrong?" James jumped when she swiftly moved from her chair to the record player and knocked it off of the shelf. He had never seen her like this before. He had never even considered her raising her voice in anger. "I'll tell you what's wrong with YOU and your mama!!!! You are both meticulously calculated evil beings! You don't think there are any consequences to your treatment of others. Well, let me enlighten you, Preacher!! Regardless of your knowledge, notoriety, position, prestige, fans, and flunkies, you will still REAP WHAT YOU HAVE SOWN!!!" Out of breath and tears swelling in her eyes, Carrington turned and ran out of the family room.

James heard her feet on the stairs, and then a door upstairs slam with such a force that the frames on the wall shook. James had never seen Carrington so angry; so hurt. Though the tears welled up in her eyes, she didn't let one fall in his presence. How did he become this person? He lost track of time, and didn't realize how long he had been sitting there with questions and thoughts swirling around in his head. James had so many questions about his mother, aunt and uncle; so many thoughts of Carrington, Tiffany, and Silas. Carrington was not coming back to finish their conversation, so James decided to just call it a night.

His legs felt like lead as he dragged himself up the stairs. Passing by Carrington's door he thought he heard sobbing. He looked at the bottom of the door frame and saw no lights on, but he knew Carrington was crying. James's own heart began to race, but something compelled him to take this chance. He said a quick prayer, and turned the door knob. He paused, briefly, but proceeded to enter the room. Carrington never heard him enter because she continued to sniffle as she lay on top of the covers of her bed. Before she could protest, James had wrapped her in his strong arms.

"Carrington, I know I have caused this pain and disappointment. Cry, Carrington. Yell, Carrington. Give me the silent treatment, but don't become me; pretending to be hard and uncaring for reasons you don't even understand. You don't have to help me with my mother, but I'm begging you, if only this one time, let me hold you so you don't cry alone in the dark. Let me catch every tear in hopes that the tears of

141

a strongly anointed, yet unappreciated, earthly angel washes away some of the dirt that's on my hands. I won't lie. Holding you is not just for you; it's helping melt away some of the coldness within my own heart." James meant every word he had spoken so much that tears were running down his own face by this time. He was glad that the only light that entered her room was that of the moon.

Carrington never said a word, but her body responded in her consent. Taking a deep breath, she slowly exhaled and fell silent. While she slept, James allowed his own tears to fall on her head. The smell of jasmine in her hair was intoxicating, and he couldn't help but pull her closer. Eventually, he fell asleep. Old things were passing away, and he could feel it.

Chapter 10

Carrington

His Confessions

Carrington woke up in a daze. She was still in her robe and lying on top of the covers. She wondered if last night had been a dream after all. She remembered coming into her room alone, and tears consistently flowing. She had cried so hard that her entire body became tired and sore. She lay down on her bed and continued to cry. Suddenly, strong arms were around her holding her so tightly that the trembling of her body was eased. She let out a deep sigh and sunk into his arms. As she began to sink further into the solace of sleep, she felt a large, yet gentle hand, caress her hair. She could feel him pull her closer and bury his face into her neck. He inhaled her, and then he began to cry. Carrington had wanted to resist and to say something, but her weariness would not allow her too. He cried, and she fell asleep in his arms. Had that been real? Had James cried as he held her? What happened to him in Atlanta? He *was* different. He was not even the same James she had fallen in love with before. He was.....who was this man?

Carrington hurriedly cleaned and dressed. She knew they needed to talk. She just wasn't sure if she was strong enough to forgive without answers. As she stepped from her room, the scent of a home cooked breakfast struck her nostrils, and her stomach indicated a need. Rounding the corner and entering the kitchen, James was putting dishes on the table in the breakfast nook. Something was definitely going on with her husband.

"James, are you alright?" Carrington didn't even attempt to hide the confusion in her voice.

Laughing, he waved his hand towards the table inviting her to come and join him for breakfast.

"Carrington, I know you think I'm only being nice because I need your help, but that's not completely true." She raised an eyebrow at him as she looked over and sniffed the prepared meal.   James continued to plead his case.

"I do want your help, but I'm being kind to you because you deserve it. Something is wrong with my mother though. There are things that my mother and family have been keeping from me. I have no one else to turn too, Carrington. Tell me; what do I need to do?"

"Eat." Caring stopped inspecting and placed her plate back on the table.

"What?" His eyebrows went up in confusion.

"Eat the food you prepared." James realized just how much Carrington distrusted him.   Instead of picking up his own fork and eating from his own plate. He took the fork she was holding from her hand and started eating from her plate.   Then, he reached for the juice that he had prepared for her and drank all of it.

"There, I'm not trying to kill you, Carrington. Really? I know I've been a jerk, but a murderer?" He couldn't believe she thought he would be that heinous.

She shrugged her shoulders and reached for the plate he had prepared for himself. "WHOOAAA! No, Ma'am, you gave your plate away." He picked up his plate and moved away from the table to the bar. As he turned away from her, he chuckled to himself.

"What?!" She had to admit, she was stubborn. Before she was pulled into his cute little game, she would fix her own breakfast. She proceeded to go to the refrigerator when he spoke again, "There's more on the stove."

"James, what happened to you in Atlanta? Why come home and start talking to me now? Why don't you just go to the Lord in the prayer? He will lead you to answers." Carrington sincerely meant what she said. She knew better now, than she ever had, that God will direct your path in the most difficult situations and give you strength to endure the journey if you believe.

"I didn't go to Atlanta, Carrington, but I did go to the Lord in prayer. He led me back to you." James was looking at her, again, with that look she didn't quite understand. "Carrington, I was right here in Michigan. I went back to my Aunt's house; Leigha, who raised me. She knows everything about my mother. Apparently, she and my uncle know more than they have ever shared with me and were about to come clean until......"

James turned away from Carrington. Dang, another door opened up to another confession that needed to be made. He didn't know how this was going to set them back. He and Carrington had just made baby steps, but this next confession could destroy any hope for them.

"James, until what? If you want my help, I need answers, and I need them today; starting now." Carrington's tone was very clear. She sounded so much like her mother that she had to look at her reflection in the stainless steel refrigerator to make sure the voice was really that of her own.

"Until the woman I had been in love with walked in as my cousin's wife. To add insult to injury, I think she's pregnant with his baby."

"The woman you're in love with? You're in love with another woman? So I have been right all this time? You don't and never have loved me!!!! Is that why you married me; to hold me hostage in this cold asylum? YOU are cruel and crazy!" Carrington was irate. She couldn't believe she had been such a fool!

"Carrington, I said I *had been* in love with this woman. You are right, okay! I married you when I was still in love with another woman, but it was not to get revenge for hurt feelings or a broken heart. Look, the more I began to get to know you, the more I liked you, but my heart belonged to her. I thought it did. You may want to sit down because I have one more confession."

"Oh, KEEP ME, JESUS. Make your confession, and then, I'm out of here. Do you hear me? I don't care if I never marry again or bust hell wide open; I'm leaving you. So talk! QUICKLY!" Carrington was livid and felt nothing but the heat of her anger rising from her body.

"Carrington, my mother made me pursue and marry you as I told you. She insisted that you were necessary for our lives. I know that is a weak excuse for what I've done, please try to understand. My mother really didn't raise me, Carrington. My Aunt Leigha, my mother's sister, and Aunt Leigha's husband, Uncle Jacob, raised me while my mother travelled the country teaching and preaching under my father's ministry to keep his legacy alive. She wanted to pass it on to me." James sat back at the breakfast nook with this distant look on his face.

"She missed a lot, but when she came to visit, she would tell me these wonderful stories about the preaching power of my father and about people she met, preached for, and even taught classes for at big conferences. My mother lavished me with attention and brought me souvenirs from all of her trips. I just wanted to please her while hoping that one day she would stay or take me with her." Coming back from his childhood thoughts, James turned his attention to Carrington. "But something is wrong. She can't even remember half of the stories she's told me. She asks me where souvenirs come from and looks puzzled when I tell her she gave them to me. And, Carrington, I know you've heard her refer to me by J.C. She's never called me by my father's initials. My father died before I was born. She has never told me the cause of his death or why she is so angry about it, but I know she carries bitterness. Please, stop staring at me like that and say something, Carrington."

Carrington straightened up her stance and walked in front of the counter that stood between her and James. Looking him straight in his eyes, with the same fire he saw in her eyes the night before, Carrington finally spoke, "I Corinthians 13:11. When I was a child, I spake as a child, I understood as a child, I thought as a child: but when I became a man, I put away childish things." Before he could say a word, she was out of the room.

As Carrington stomped her way upstairs, too angry to cry, she thought about what an idiot she had been. What had she missed? Was it all just an act? Why would God allow such deceit?

Entering her room, she began to pull everything from her dressers and stuffing things in suitcases. She was snatching clothing off of hangers, when her eyes fell on the solid white garment bag; the wedding dress. Carrington fell to her knees right there in her closet.

"God, I am so sorry. I know I disobeyed my mother's wishes, but did I sin against You too. I saw You in his walk. I heard You in his speech. I felt You in his touch. Was it all lies and deceit of the enemy? Was it lustful desires that blinded me from the truth and deafened me to Your warning? Father, what does this mean about us? Do I not know You or recognize Your voice as I thought I did? Abba......Abba......Abba, please, forgive me. Forgive my attitude; forgive my defiance; forgive my lust, and show me. Show me Your Truth, My Lord, please."

She wasn't sure how long she had been on the floor of her closet. Carrington only remembered praying until her knees hurt. She must have prayed and cried herself to sleep. As she stood to her feet, she looked around her closet. It was completely empty. No shoes; no hangers; no sweaters remained. Everything was gone, and that included the wedding dress. She stumbled out of her closet still a little dazed. On her bed were her suitcases neatly lined up and full. There was a piece of James's stationary on top of one of her bags. Carrington recognized his penmanship.

Carrington,

I know you must hate me, and I don't blame you. I've been lying to you since the day we met, and there is no way I can ever make that up to you. I have taken your advice. I went to God after I visited my family, and I prayed an earnest prayer. I'm still praying. I have asked for God's forgiveness, and now I ask for your forgiveness. I've told you all of the truth as I know it, but there is so much more that I don't know. I don't know why my mother wanted this, but I do know now that it comes from a dark place and is not your problem. You owe me nothing.

I finished packing for you, and I've transferred money into a private account with only your name on it. Money could never repay you for what you have endured at the hands of my mother and I, but it will take care of you until you decide what you want. I pray that you get everything you have dreamed of because your

153

heart deserves it. All of your banking information is in your duffel bag. The keys to the Bentley are beside your purse. It's your car. I will never forget you, Carington Rebekah Mitchell.

Carrington opened the duffel bag James mentioned in his letter. There was a green envelop lying on top of her belongings. She dropped the folder on the floor and gasped. She couldn't believe him. She quickly scooped up the folder to look again at the starting deposit. James had deposited $50,000 into a private account that belonged to her only. Looking out of her window and holding on to the folder, Carington started thinking about her own relationship with her mother. Her mother's forgiveness had come to her so easily. Even after her only child whom she had cared for with everything she had, had directly defied her and walked away without a word for five years she forgave. She remembered the Scripture, "Father, forgive us our trespasses as we forgive those who trespass against us."

"James!" Carrington raced down the stairs and found James on the back deck. At the sound of her voice, he quickly jumped up from his patio chair and faced her.

"What's wrong?" James looked frightened and confused.

"I have never wanted your money. James, all I ever wanted was for you to love me as Christ loves the church. That's all HE expects, and all I wanted, but I don't trust you anymore. You have to earn that back if you want any type of relationship with me. I won't be purchased and neither will my love and trust, but I will help you figure out what's going on." Carrington handed him back the green folder. I'll help you."

"Carrington, the account belongs to you. Do what you want with your money, but I won't take it back. I am so grateful for your forgiveness and help." James stepped toward her to embrace her in a hug, but Carrington stepped back.

"Time, James. I do forgive you, but it's going to take time to move from where we are right now. Where do we start with this whole mystery?" James was determined to respect her wishes.

"I've called my Aunt Leigha and asked if she and my uncle could come here to talk. They should be here later this evening. Will you join us? We don't have to pretend to be the happy couple, but I would really appreciate not having to hear whatever confessions they need to make alone."

"That's fine on one condition." He may have needed Carrington, but Carrington needed someone else at her side.

"Anything, Carington. Just tell me; I owe you."

"My mother is coming. I allowed your schemes to hurt our relationship, James, and she deserves an explanation. She knew something was wrong from the start."

"Okay, Carrington, you don't have to explain. Call her, and I'll secure her transportation." James hoped he did well with hiding his fear of seeing Tilda again.

Carrington couldn't wait to see her mother, but she was terrified about her mother's reaction when she learned the truth. She had a sinking feeling in her gut that said, everyone was about to be shook before all was settled. Turning back to enter the house to contact her mother, Carrington looked over her shoulder at James.

"James, I'm going to call my mother. You should start praying again."

Chapter 11

James

Trauma Has a Long Reach

James was like a nervous school boy. He had not really thought the invitation to his aunt and uncle through. James knew whatever they needed to reveal was going to be heavy, and he didn't know how he would react. One thing he was sure of was that Carrington was going to be there. He was so grateful she had agreed to stay and help him sort out what was going on with his mother. Once again, James could see the genuine heart of Carrington; a heart she never withheld from people. He hated how he had used and hurt her. His mind started to roam down a "what if" trail, but it was brought to a dead halt at the sound of the doorbell. His Aunt Leigha and Uncle Jacob had arrived.

Exiting from the room, James heard Carrington's voice greeting their guest. Each step he took downstairs was filled with nervousness, but he had prayed for the Lord to prepare his heart for what was to be received from his guardians. James was determined to help his mother, and he understood that he needed the facts to ensure that he did just that.

"Hi, Uncle Jacob and Aunt Leigha. Welcome to our home." James shook his uncle's hand and hugged his aunt in the usual greeting.

The couples sat down in the formal living room across from one another. The atmosphere was extremely tense and uncomfortable, and James didn't have the energy to think about how to settle it.

"Maybe we should pray." Carrington had no premeditated plan concerning this meeting, but she knew that the presence of the Lord was needed. No one agreed or disagreed, so she proceeded to pray for the communication to honest and clear and for the forgiveness, healing, and unity of the family. By the time she finished, a peace had settled over all of them.

"James, we came to be honest with you concerning your mother's health. First, please understand that we love you and your mother, and the decisions we made were to honor your mother's wishes." Uncle Jacob talked as if his mother were dead. Her wishes? What was he talking about?

"Uncle Jacob, are you trying to say my mother is dying? What do you mean by her wishes?" James felt a familiar fear rising up in him.

Leigha spoke up. "James, your mother is not dying, but she is very sick. Before we came here, we did a little investigating because we were very concerned after your visit." Tears begin to flow down his aunt's face, but her voice remained strong. "James, your mother is suffering and has been since she was about sixteen. Your mother is the only living witness to our father raping me."

"I had been molested by our father since I was seven years old. It all escalated as I grew up. Lorna was just like him; headstrong so they were very close, but he often took me away from the house on "special dates" when my mother and Lorna were around. When they were away, he had his way with me at home, but that particular day he was angry because he saw your Uncle Jacob walk me home. He hated any boy that showed interest in me and had run many away, but Jacob refused to go. He was enraged when I walked in the house and immediately grabbed me. He started yelling and hitting me. Then, the sexual assault happened. He knew where my mother was, but he didn't know that Lorna had skipped school, again, and was in the basement of our home. She heard the banging and my screams, and came running through the back door of the house. I guess she was going to pretend she had come from school, but she was shocked by what she witnessed." Jacob reached out and grasped his wife's hand. This is the first time, he had learned of the details surrounding his wife's rape.

"What? Aunt Leigha, I can't imagine. I'm so......I'm so sorry. James empathized with his aunt, but was still so confused. "Please understand that my heart breaks for you, but I still don't understand what this has done to my mother."

"James, our father was Lorna's heart. That day he left our home and us for good. Lorna begged him not to go or to take her with him, but he told her that because of what I had made him do, he could never stay. Two traumatic experiences for a teenage girl. Her hero raped her sister, and then, left her. Soon, Lorna was different. She became fixated on having the perfect family when she grew up. She started pretending she was rich, and our parents travelled all of the time because our father was a famous preacher."

This was a lot for James to hear. He could feel Carrington's eyes on him, but his head felt too heavy to lift. Famous travelling preacher? These were like stories she told him about his father.

"She only went to school because mother did her assignments for her. My mother tried to get her help, but didn't know where to take her without embarrassing her. We were well known because of our father. Your mother stole credit cards and falsified applications to get credit cards and loans in my and our mother's names. I couldn't take it anymore. I left home, and married your uncle. Lorna made it known that she hated me because in her mind I was doing everything I could to stop her from having the perfect family. She blamed me for our father leaving."

Perfect family? He had heard this reference from his mother so many times. She was determined that he would give her the perfect family. What was he hearing? What was wrong with his mother?

"James, please know I'm telling you this because my sister is very sick, but I know, with the right help, she can live a good life. She has been diagnosed with Schizophrenia. I don't understand a lot about it, but I know there is help. She's been in a good facility, and until recently, we have had no problems with her there."

"Facility? What facility? She's been in some type of crazy house all this time? That can't be true." James couldn't take sitting there quietly anymore. "They wouldn't just let her leave like that. She pops up here anytime she wants too. How do you explain that, Aunt Leigha?"

"James, recently the care facility where I placed my sister was bought out and new management took place. They overhauled the old staff and brought in new hires. Because the older staff was less technologically up-to-date, they kept paper files on the residents. Some of these files or parts of files where misplaced during the restructuring of the facility. Information gets lost physically and in translation when you are going from one way of documentation and storage to a totally new computer system and data collection procedures. Your mother has always had the skill of persuasion. She showed them what she needed them to see to get the results she wanted. They gave her more leniency than the previous staff. She now gets weekend and holiday passes. A care facility nurse has been escorting her under the impression that all is well. They believed that you didn't visit because Lorna had asked you not too, and you agreed to have her in your home whenever she came to visit." His aunt handed him a sheet of paper stating all that she had just explained signed by what appeared to be his signature and that of a lawyer he didn't even know. "They received a signed and notarized copy of this statement from you and your lawyer."

" I knew you didn't do this. That's her money-hungry lawyer's work." Leigha explained.

"I have her home number. I call her live-in housekeeper to make sure that she gets home safely. I've talked to this woman. Her name is Erin. " James mind could not but help but question how insane his mother had to be to go through such lengths for revenge.

Leigha took a deep breath and exhaled before answering, "James, you have her personal facility care nurse's work number. That's who you have been speaking too."

"This is so unbelievable, Aunt Leigha. Why didn't you tell me? Why did you let her feel my head with all the lies?" Now, tears were running down James's face. Carrington sat there amazed by all she heard. This was something out of a movie. She now felt a deep sense of pain for James. He was definitely reaping what he had sown, but she prayed for God's grace and mercy to be poured on him. How much could one take?

"James, your mother was happiest when she was able to be with you. Your love for her brought a glow to her that no one has ever been able to do sense that horrible day she faced. And you, Son, you beamed when she walked in the room. You always knew you were an important part of our family, but nothing compared to being in your own mother's presence."

Jacob was trying his best to give James some relief. James saw a pained look on his aunt's face at the last statement her husband made. When she realized James's gaze was still focused on her, she quickly looked away.

"I don't know what's real anymore. I don't know what to say or how I am supposed to feel." James stood up and walked to the ceiling-to-floor window overlooking the lake.

Perhaps it was a wife's instinct, but Carrington knew he needed to know she was still there. She walked to his right side, and placed her hand in the middle of his back. He was deep in his own thoughts and jumped at her touch. He looked down into her big shining eyes, and felt peace move within himself. Carrington. His Carrington. She was real. How did she play apart in this mess? Why had she and her mother been targeted?

James turned on his heels to face his aunt and uncle once again. "Aunt Leigha, who is my father?"

Leigha jumped up from her seat, but she must have been a bit overwhelmed by this meeting also, because just as soon as she was on her feet, she fainted. Jacob was on the floor by her side in lightening speed; gently shaking her and calling her name. Leigha was not out long, but Jacob refused to allow her to move forward in the conversation. James desperately wanted an answer, but understood his uncle's stance. The two men guided Leigha to another guest suite to rest for the afternoon while Carrington prepared her lavender tea to help her relax and rest.

As Carrington waited on the water to heat for the tea, she was chilled by James's question. Who is my father? The same exact question she asked her own mother so many times as she grew up. The sore spot. This void. The emptiness, that be explained, of not knowing the other half of your genetic make-up was shared by she and James.

Chapter 12
Carrington
There's a Storm Coming

Carrington hired a chef to cook all of her mother's favorite southern foods. As she was enjoying the delicious smells coming from her own stove and ovens, she heard a car pull into the driveway. It could not have been her mother because she wasn't due to the evening. She started toward the foyer when she heard keys at the door. No way. There was only one other person, besides she and James, with a key to this house. Carrington stood still as Lady Lorna entered her home like she lived there too. She could not have had worse timing. Carrington knew there was a storm out on the ocean moving towards them at record speed, but she certainly was not expected it to show up today.

"Are you going to stand there like an imbecile or assist me with my luggage?"

Lady Lorna was her usual rude self upon arrival.

"I thought James explained that we would see you in a few weeks during the Christmas holidays. Why are you here, Lorna?" Knowing what she knew now, Carrington wasn't as intimidated as she had been and kind of felt sorry for Lorna. She tried to speak to her calmly and with gentleness.

"I am *his* mother, young lady. I grew tired of being alone and wanted to be home with my son." Lorna picked up one of her bags and dropped it at Carrington's feet. "Now, if you don't mind, I would like to go to my quarters to rest before dinner."

"Lorna, we have guests, and you need to know that some information has surfaced that we need to deal with immediately since you are back. Please, stay here and allow me to go get James." Carrington started for James's study where he had retreated after she assured him she would take care of Uncle Jacob and Aunt Leigha. She prayed that they would at least stay out of sight while she went to get James. No assumptions could be made at the reaction Lorna would have seeing her sister and brother-in-law at her son's home.

"I most certainly will not! What is going on here? You seem a bit relaxed in speaking to me today." Apparently, Lorna noticed Carrington dismissing her title when she called her name. "Where is all of this talk of "we" suddenly coming from, and where is my son; the sole owner of this home and everything in it?" This struck a nerve.

Carrington decided, at that moment, not to seek James until she had a word with her mother-in-law privately. "Lady Lorna, where are my manners. It's been quite a morning. I apologize for my tone and behavior, please, let me help you to your room." Carrington would play this game for a few minutes.

Carrington stepped aside and allowed Lorna to enter first. When they were both inside the room, Carrington threw each of Lorna's bags into a corner on the floor one by one. Lorna's mouth dropped open in shock.

Knowing her next move, Carrington stepped in front of the door blocking her exit.

"What is this? MOVE! I'm going to find James and let him know that you are out of your mind!" Lorna made the threat, but did not make a move toward Carrington. Her heart racing, Carrington realized that, for once, she had the upper hand.

"You are not going to leave this room. Lorna there is, indeed, something going on. That something is all centered on you. Now, my husband has had a very trying morning so I will go and tell him of your defiant presence in OUR home. Let me make one other thing clear. Your son, my husband, is the sole owner of this home and everything in it. BUT make no mistake, when he made me his wife without a prenuptial agreement, freely he gave and freely I will receive if he should decide to stay with your way of thinking." Leaving Lorna with her mouth, again, gapped open, Carrington walked out of the room. As she hurried toward James's study, she couldn't help but smile. She might be clueless about her biological father, but she was definitely her mother's daughter.

She entered his study ready to alert him of his mother's arrival, but realized he was praying. She stood in the doorway of his office and quietly waited for him to complete his talk with God. Without a word, he held out his hand to her. How did he know it was her who had come? She cautiously moved to his side and took his hand. She couldn't hear a word come from his mouth, but knew he had included her in his prayer. Finishing, he stood up and invited her to take a seat.

"James, your mother has come back. She's in her room right now." Carrington didn't want to sit down; she wanted him to do something.

"What?! Has she seen my aunt and uncle?" His expression confirmed that keeping her in her room had been a good idea on Carrington's part. "I really didn't want this to happen like this, but the truth is knocking on our door. I'll go let her know that they are here. Will you let Aunt Leigha and Uncle Jacob know she is here for me?"

"Yes." Carrington started toward the door when another horrifying thought came to mind. "James, my mother is on her way. She will be here by dinner."

"God is with us, Carrington, but it's going to get worse before it gets better. You do know this, don't you?"

"Yes, but God is bigger than the storm that we are about to face." Carrington exited his study and headed toward the guest suite. James followed closely behind her to face his mother. Right as he shut his study door, he heard his name.

"James! That woman has lost her ever-lacking mind. She's been rude and disrespectful since I came in the door; talking to me like she's crazy. Tell her who I am?" Lorna was fuming. If she wasn't sick, Carrington would be on the floor. Lorna was BIG-BIG mad.

"Mother, how respectful was it for you not to let us prepare for your coming? It's alright, though, you're here now. Let's go talk in your quarters." They turned their backs to Carrington as they walked back to Lorna's room, and just as Carrington continued to go warn their other guests, Aunt Leigha came from her room.

"Lorna? Lorna is that you, Baby Sis?" Leigha started to make her way toward Lorna and James from the other side of the hall.

"Leigha? Leigha, why are you here? Why are you in my son's home?" Carrington knew someone should intervene, but neither she nor James could move. What was about to happen was lost on both of them.

"Lorna, we came to see about you, Baby. Lorna, have you stopped taking your medicine again? You should be at home." Anyone could see the concern on Leigha's face, but Lorna looked brutishly at her sister.

Leigha moved to embrace her little sister and was met with a terrifyingly striking slap across her face. Lorna slapped Leigha so fiercely that Leigha fell against the wall and slid to the floor in a puddle. Carrington raced to her side. Jacob ran into the hall, and he and Lorna's eyes locked. He looked down at the floor and moved into action when he saw Leigha there.

"Leigha, Baby."

Lorna looked disgusted and walked into her room.

"James, I'm going to rest before dinner." With that said, she slammed the door in his face before he could utter a word of chastisement.

Jacob and Carrington gathered Leigha from the floor for the second time. She was distraught even more than she was when James had asked about his father; a question still unanswered. They walked her back to the guest room.

"Sweetheart, are you alright. We should go and just call someone from the new care facility to come and pick her up. She's become too violent." Jacob was truly concerned for his wife. Carrington remained quiet trying to wait for information to be revealed. She went into the restroom to soak a towel to put on Leigha's bruising face.

"No, Jacob. I'm tired of seeing my sister go through this. The truth has to come out; all of it. I need to tell my sister what she saw happen to me was real, and it was NOT her fault, and she needs to tell James the truth about his existence. We both have, no, we all have truths that we need to hear and handle. Maybe, then, my sister can begin to heal. Jacob you preach it, but we have not lived it. The truth shall set us free. I don't care how long it takes. I'm not leaving here until it's all out." Leigha sounded a lot stronger than she seemed. The love Leigha felt for her sister could be heard in her voice. Carrington could see how the love of God had healed the damage that trauma had caused Leigha, and in turn, Leigha desperately tried to give her sister that same healing love. What does a child make of seeing their hero committing such a terrifying act against another child? Carrington could not help but feel compassion for Lorna; she was broken.

Carrington re-entered the bedroom and told Leigha to hold the cold towel to her cheek.

"There you go. Maybe that will help with the bruising. You guys just relax. If you need anything you can call downstairs. I'll be in the kitchen with the chef, so I'll hear you from there. When dinner is ready, I'll call you." Carrington turned to leave them with privacy.

"Carrington," Leigha spoke up, "I'm not sure what you have heard or what you know. I do know you can't know too much because James doesn't really know the facts. I'm trying to ask you not to judge James because of where he comes from or us because of the choices we've made to protect him. Lorna, Jacob, and I have also made, what I now see to be, selfish choices to protect our own hearts and images. I know that the truth to be revealed is going to be mighty painful, Carrington, but it is going to set us free from the bondage of lies and deceit. He's going to need you. James is going to need someone real; someone true. Someone who refuses to pretend and loves him for who he is rather than what he does or what he aspires to do. Please promise me that you will stay with him."

Looking into Leigha's eyes, Carrington saw the genuine love this woman carried for her family. Yet, Carrington had to be true to herself and honest with Leigha.

"Aunt Leigha, the love you have for your family is undeniably sincere. You're a good person, and I will not lie to you. I can't promise you that I will be that woman for James. I don't know who he really is, and he has deceived me. There are things that I have just found out before you all came. I am here now, and while I'm here I'm going to support him." Not wanting to prolong the conversation, Carrington exited the room as quickly as she could.

The kitchen felt like a safe haven. Carrington sampled the food she was having prepared and all tasted perfect. Regardless of whatever else might go wrong, at least the food would be right. Carrington didn't know which way the evening would turn when Tilda and Lorna met for the first time. Now, knowing that Lorna was struggling mentally, Carrington didn't even really know if she wanted Tilda to meet Lorna. She decided to stay out of sight and pray until dinner was ready.

Before Carrington could escape the madness and go to her room, James came downstairs. He looked so tired; zombie-like. He didn't look in Carrington's direction. Sitting at the breakfast corner, he stared out of the window. As much as she wanted to just walk away, something was pushing toward her husband.

"James, are you alright?" She hoped this would not start a long conversation. She didn't have the energy right now.

"I've lied to you enough, Carrington. No, I'm not alright. After convincing my mother to rest, when she fell asleep I went through her things. I found unopened bottles of medication. I found where she perfected my signature and signed letters that I never wrote providing her permission to be released under my care. The only thing she was honest about is her money. She has plenty of money which I'm assuming is how she hired this crook of a lawyer. I found his card. I just need to digest all of this, Carrington, so that I can make the best decisions for my mother. Better days are coming; they have too. I'm going for a walk; see you at dinner. Thanks, again, Carrington."

James got up from the table and headed toward the front door. Carrington knew it was praying time. James had no idea that things were going to hurt much worse before his healing would begin. She hoped that she could also endure.

Chapter 13

Tilda vs. Lorna
Meeting of the Mothers

Tilda could not believe she was on her way to see her daughter. It had been far too long, and her heart was racing. She didn't know why she was so nervous or if she would be able to hide it. Tilda had been up for a day and a half trying to make sure she had all that she needed for this trip. Pastor was so concerned that he called Vicki and paid her to take time off from work to go with Tilda. Vicki was too excited. She was just glad to be going out of town with her best friend again; even if she didn't understand Tilda's nervousness.

Tilda didn't know how Carrington was going to react to Vicki's presence, but it didn't matter because Vicki was not going anywhere. Not knowing what she would find or how she and James would interact, she was glad for the company. Tilda had not told

Vicki that she was really eager to see Lady Lorna and kept her promise to her daughter. She had not even told Vicki about her and Caring's conversation. Telling Vicki would be like giving her permission to interrogate this Lady Lorna. Meanwhile, Lorna was making her dissatisfaction with dinner known to Carrington.

"I see you decided to go back to your roots via dinner." Lady Lorna was back to using her flippant mouth and annoying sarcasm.

She did not realize that Carrington was about to take her back to her roots deeper than she had ever dared before. Lorna honestly didn't know what to make of this newfound confidence and no-nonsense attitude. Where did it come from all of a sudden? She overheard her tell James that the rest of their company would arrive in ten minutes. Why did she and James seem so different? It was almost like they were a real couple.

Suddenly, the doorbell began to ring repeatedly. Carrington dashed from the kitchen before Lorna could stand from her chair in the formal living room. She made it to the door right before Lady rounded the corner.

"Heeeeyyyyyyyy, GIRLLLLLL!!!!! Su- PRISE!!!!", shouted Vicki as Carrington stood in the door staring at her in utter shock!

"Auntie Vicki? What are you doing here? Where's my mama?" Carrington had not been expecting to see her Auntie.

She definitely didn't know how this was going to play out. Auntie Vicki was the kind that would climb across the dining room table and reach out to touch Lady Lorna if the wrong look was given or the wrong word was said.

"Un-Uhhhhh! Is that how they talk to they aunties up here in Mitch-a-gain? RUDE!!! You ain't been raised like that Cari. MOVE!" Vicki spoke as she crossed the threshold of the door and gently moved Carrington out of her way. "Yo, Mama sitting out there in the car praying, Honey. I told her she could do that while we blessed the food.

I'm hungry, Gul, and my back hurt. Fix me a plate of whatever I'm smelling, and get me some I-b-profen. Hurry up, now."

"Uh, yes, Ma'am. Does Mama need help with her bags?" Carrington knew not to try her auntie by correcting her behavior or speech, so she did what she was raised to do; follow directions.

"Naw, not right now. You know she ain't coming in until she finished talking to the Lort."

"Excuse me", Lorna interjected while Vicki was quiet, "Carrington, who is this….person who has just forced her way into my son's home?"

"Oh, Help, Jesus", Carrington whispered under her breathe.

"Who she talking about, Cari? She talking about me?" Carrington, out of fear, could only nod her head in affirmation. "MU-AH?"

Carrington knew her Auntie Vicki was about to read Lady Lorna up one side and down the other; she braced herself.

"Well, tell Ms. THANG that this person is the person that ain't in the mood for no boo-gee foolishness cause my feet hurt; my back hurt; and I'm hungry!!! Now, Cari, don't make me say it again. I know you rich now, so call Benton to fix me a plate!"

"Ghetto foolishness is better than class and dignity in your feeble little mind, I assume. You are rude and wrong. I am what is referred to as sophisticated. Also, understand, Carrington is NOT rich, but my son is very well off as you can see."

Carrington could see Lorna stick her chest out a little bit more. She had to give it to Lorna; she was standing her ground. For now that is, but Carrington wasn't sure how long she would last.

"LLLLLLL-OOOOK, Lady!!! You 'bout to make me forfeit my place in Heaven standing over there looking like a new Slim

Jim. I WILL bite you!!! And for the record, you are a.....

"Hey, Auntie! Let me show you to the dining room.   You can sit down and rest while we prepare your plate."   Carrington walked between the ladies and took Vicki by the hand.   She held her tight as they left Lorna stewing in the foyer.

Lorna headed towards James's study when the front door opened again.   Who could it be this time, and why had Carrington invited these people to her son's home? Surely, James's didn't know she was inviting these types of people.

She turned back towards the door and came face-to-face with the one who was her true nemesis and fueled her rage.   Tilda Larain Mitchell. Lorna felt like someone had sucked the air from her when she saw *the* coat.   The same red coat in her nightmares. The same red coat from the night her husband was murdered.

Tilda could not believe her eyes.   It was Lady Jay. Lady Jay Hewman was staring at her as if she had seen a ghost. How in the world? Tilda had not seen her since she was pregnant with Carrington.

"Lady Jay?"

Lorna was snapped from the past with the sound of the name she used in Alabama as First Lady of Holy Ghost Fulfillment Baptist Church. Tilda Larain Mitchell had captured her husband's eye from the first time he saw her. She was young, but she was beautiful and that was his weakness. He had temporarily satisfied the appetite of his demons with other women in the church, but Lady Lorna knew who he really wanted to devour. He had an appetite like her father's so she recognized the signs and had found evidence in their own home. She could have cared less as long as he played the role scripted for him so that their perfect family could excel past her father's accomplishments and stand with the Who's Who of the religious community. Tilda destroyed that with her accusations, and J. C. had been messy with this one.

"My name is Lady Lorna now. Hello, Tilda Mitchell. I've been waiting for this for a *very* long time. Have you come to rescue your daughter or have you come to face your own demons?"

"Lady Lorna? What are you talking about? And yes, since you brought her up. Why are you making my daughter's life miserable? That's not a safe move, Lady-Whomever-You-Are-Today."

Tilda was even more confused, but she was completely confident that this was a part of a bigger and sicker plan. She just didn't know who had devised it or where it was headed, but she did know it was coming to an end.

"My middle initial starts with "J". Hence the name "Jay". My husband was fonder of my middle name then, so I used the name Lady Jay; short for Lady Jazeebel. I wasn't expecting you until later in the game, but since you are here, Tilda, you will reap what you have sown soon enough. You broke my family, and I'm going to break your demon seed once and for all. I hope you will be staying a while. We have so much to talk about and share with the *children*."

Lorna cautiously walked past Tilda and ascended the stairs. This was going to better than she imagined. Now, she could torture mother and daughter until mommy broke and had to admit what she had done. James would be hurt for a moment about being used, but it wasn't like he had slept with the girl. He would get over it when he realized what they had taken from him. The game had just gone to another level.

"Mama, are you alright?" Carrington emerged from the dining room to find Tilda looking towards the stairs with a confused expression on her face. Following her gaze, Carrington caught the back of Lady Lorna's figure rounding the corner to go to James's study. What had she missed?

"Mama, what did she say to you?" Carrington felt a heat rise in her that she had not experienced before. Lady Lorna could demean her all she wanted, but hell would freeze over before she allowed her to disrespect her mother.

"My baby. My sweet girl or should I refer to you as a beautiful young lady? Look at you." Tilda would have to put Lorna out of her mind for the rest of the night. This was her first night in her daughter's home, and she did not want to upset Carrington. She was sure that she and Lorna would have their day. Something told her that Lorna was going to make sure of that.

"I guess you can say I get it from my Mama", Carrington smiled looking into her mother's beautiful eyes.

She could see exactly what she would look like when she was older, and she wasn't mad about it. Her mother has aged, but still extremely beautiful, and she was a splendid replica of that beauty.

"Come on, Mama. Let me show you to your room. Do you want your own quarters or would you and Auntie Vicki prefer to share?" Carrington took hold of her mother's rolling suitcase with one hand and her mother's hand with her other.

"Oh, I had not thought about what 'quarters' I would prefer. Where I'm from you did well if you had a bed by yourself, but I see you are way past that." Tilda could not help but notice the grandeur her daughter lived in now.

"Mama, I'm only asking if you want a guest room to yourself or if you and Auntie want to share a room. I just want you to be comfortable. It's no big deal."

"Caring, I'm sorry. You don't have to apologize for having this impeccable home. I wasn't trying to embarrass you or make you feel bad." Tilda knew her daughter loved and respected her, and she wanted Caring to know the feeling was mutual. There was nothing that could make her withhold her love from her child.

"You better give us a room we can share. You know how your Auntie Vicki is about being in new places. Besides, I will need to keep an eye on her if you want to ensure the safety of little Lady Lorna." The two ladies shared a laugh as they entered one of the guest rooms in the house.

"Mom, why don't you put your things away and wash up for dinner. Auntie is already in the dining room sampling to keep her nerves calm. She and Lady Lorna got off on the wrong foot. Dinner will be ready by the time you come down." Carrington placed her mom's suitcase on one of the beds in the room and started back towards the door. "I hope you're hungry because all of your favorite foods have been prepared to your liking."

"Thank you so much, Sweetie, but you really didn't have to go through the trouble. I'm just glad to lay eyes on you." This was the truth. It wasn't all the truth, but it was the main part of the truth. Carrington looked a lot stronger and healthier since Tilda seen her at the boutique.

"I love you, Mama. I really love you for always being honest with me even if you were telling me things I didn't want to hear. Thank you." Carrington exited the room to allow her mom a moment to unpack.

Always being honest. Those words were like daggers to Tilda's heart. Tilda knew something was coming that was going to test their relationship even more so than James's defiance and deceit. If she only knew exactly what it was, she could figure out what to say to Carrington to warn her or help her during the trial.

Oh, well, she thought. That will have to wait. Tonight she was going to enjoy the dinner her baby had prepared in her honor. Tilda began to unpack and get settled in for the next couple of weeks. She had no idea how long two weeks could seem.

Chapter 14
Tilda and Lorna
A Mother Faulting Showdown

Dinner was ready. Carrington felt uneasiness in the pit of her belly. She turned off her bathroom light ready to exit her room when she heard a light tap on her door. She figured it was her mother and opened the door without inquiring. It was James, and he looked and smelled better than the food waiting for them.

"James. Um, Um, I was just headed toward the dining room." Carrington was having a hard time looking into those beautiful eyes. She was reminded of the man that captivated her attention from the beginning.

"Good; so am I. May I escort my wife to our table?" That smile.

Carrington felt herself being drawn in but forced herself to resist. NO! This was the same man that had courted and married her while being in love with someone else just to please his evil behaving mother.

"Carrington, I know I'm not on your list of family and friends, but please don't keep hating me. This is not for a show or act. I just want to make it clear that you are to be respected in your home." James meant every word he had spoken. Carrington deserved to be respected, and she would receive nothing less in his presence while she remained in their home.

Carrington took his arm, and they made their way to dinner. They didn't say another word to one another on their decent downstairs. When they reached the bottom, Carrington stopped him.

"James, before we walk in here I need to tell you something." Carrington felt the Spirit urging her to warn him. "The truth does set us free from the things that are holding us captive to sin and keeping us from growing in the Lord. Often, the truth hurts first because a breaking must take place. Before you can enjoy a new bottle of wine, the cork, or seal, must be broken. Before we can enjoy gifts at Christmas, the beautiful wrapping is ripped off. James, more pain is coming, but remember, it is the beginning of your healing process. Sometimes the pain endured is the key to open the door to abundant blessings."

"Carrington, you're absolutely right, and I have asked God to prepare my heart and mind. I have no doubt that there will be much pain, but I have every confidence that my God is more powerful than any measure of it. Because of His power, I will endure. I receive your words and heed your warning. Thank you for staying with me through this storm." There was no more that could be said. She obeyed the Lord, and James received His word. She did not know this word was also for her.

"GIRL, I'M HANGRY!!! Hungry and angry about it! What are we waiting on ?!" Vicki was speaking to Tilda but could be heard throughout the house. James could hear this loud woman before he set eyes on her and looked at Carrington.

"That's my Aunt Vicki. I didn't know my mother was bringing her," she apologetically explained.

James laughed, "This should be interesting."

The first thing Carrington noticed was the look on Lorna's face when she and James entered the room. She was in disbelief. Lorna's face showed pure agony when James pulled Carrington's chair out for her to sit down right beside him. Anger took over her face when Leigha and Jacob entered the room, and James asked Jacob to take the other end of the table with Leigha to his side. Tilda sat between Carrington and Vicki. The empty chair next to Lorna provided the space needed between her and Leigha. With everyone seated, James surprisingly asked his mother-in-law to bless the food. Tilda at first was stunned, but quickly gathered her thoughts and did as she was asked.

Before Tilda could begin, Lorna spoke, "Yes, a good prayer is going to be needed. Tilda, please say a word for my enemies." She took James's hand and bowed her head. Tilda continued on with the blessing.

Dinner was strained. There was so much tension in the air and so many questions without answers loomed over the table. It seemed as if everyone held their breath as they ate. Everyone except Lorna. She stared continuously at Tilda throughout dinner. As dishes became empty and were cleared from the table, Tilda finally broke the silence.

"Uh, Caring, Mama is whooped, Baby. I think I'm going to head to bed. James, I appreciate you allowing us into your home and the dinner. Pastor Jacob and Leigha, it was nice meeting you." Tilda spoke not one word to Lorna but did give a stone glare.

"You are more than welcome, Pastor." Carrington turned to James. He had never shown much respect for her mother or her mother's calling to pastorship. "This is our home, and you are Carrington's mother; therefore, welcome any time."

Tilda nodded her thanks, and begin to get up from the table. For a second, Carrington thought that it would be a peaceful dinner after all. She thought too soon.

"Carrington, did your mother tell you that we knew one another?" Lady Lorna spoke without looking up at Carrington.

This wasn't anything out of the ordinary for Carrington. She was used to being treated with disregard, but she was more concerned with what Lady Lorna was about to speak.

"Excuse, me? You know my mother?" Carrington didn't understand how that was possible or why Tilda had not said something earlier. "Mama, you already knew Lorna?"

"Excuse, me. I do not know Lady Lorna. I know Lady Jay Hewman." Tilda made herself comfortable once again.

She knew a battle had begun. She looked right at Carrington as she spoke. She turned toward Lorna awaiting her response.

She wanted to know what problem Lorna had with her that would cause her to mistreat Carrington and put herself in such danger.

"Well, how do you two know each other?" Carrington could sense that not only had they met previously, but they did not care for each other to say the least.

"Yes, Tilda, do tell how we know one another. I'm sure both of our children will be in for a big surprise." Lady Lorna suddenly put down her fork, and stared at Tilda with a hard stare.

"You don't want to go there, Ms. Lady. How about you just tell me what your problem is so that I can help you rectify it, and you can get out of my daughter's life. This way everyone stays safe."

Carrington could see the stark difference between her and her mother. Her mother was not afraid or intimidated by anyone.

"YOU KILLED MY HUSBAND!!!!" Lady Lorna was on her feet and screaming at Tilda. "YOU did it, and I saw you!! You took away my dreams and destroyed my family. Then, you spread lies that forced me to leave town as you tried to ruin my husband's legacy!!!" She was hysterical. "She took your father away from you, James, that's why I gave you her daughter!"

"Who IS you yelling at? YOU, Ma'am. Who is YOU yelling at?" Tilda had long since put up her boxing gloves, but Vicki kept her gloves on and carried a spare pair. Vicki started dabbing the corners of her mouth and taking off of her earrings. Then, she picked up her fork.

Carrington didn't know how to respond to such an accusation. Seeing the matter was about to become much worse, she turned to face her aunt in hopes of deescalating the situation.

"Auntie, please put the fork back on your plate and calm down."

"Caring, only because I love you, and I don't want your Mammy to start some looooong prayer, BUT you betta change your tone and lower your voice, Lady LOONEY." Carrington breathed a sigh of relief.

At that point, James looked up in sheer disbelief. "You killed my father?"

"Oh, Lord. Carrington, do you have any to-go boxes?" Vicki knew something was about to go down. "This was a terrible idea. Whose idea was this anyway? That's the person I ought to juke with this fork."

"HOW DARE YOU!!! I have never killed anyone, but you are right not to put it past me! You sound crazy! Do you even know who your husband was and what he did?" Tilda could feel her temper trying to take over, but she had to hold it together. Carrington did not know the circumstances surrounding her birth, and this is not how Tilda intended for her to find out.

"You killed my father?" James's eyes were focused on his mother-in-law as he leaned toward here. "Why?"

Lorna cut in, "I know exactly who my husband was because my father and I groomed him. Of course, I knew about his sexual transgressions. I couldn't hold that against him. What man would not have fallen into temptation with the likes of harlots running through the church? You were all after him. Hopping around every Sunday trying to gain his attention with your shouting and tongue-speaking. He was going places, and I was not about to let anyone ruin that for us. BUT YOU!"

"What did you say?" Tilda felt a familiar anger rise in her that she had not experienced in a very long time. She stopped trying to fight it. "You KNEW?"

"COME ON IN THE ROOM!!! OOOOOHHHHH, COME ON IN THE ROOM!!! JESUS, WE GONE NEED A DOCTOR! COME ON IN THE ROO-OOM!" Vicki was out of her chair and rocking like she was in a choir stand.

"What's going on?" Carrington felt a fear rising within her. She had been clueless about this animosity between the two mothers. "Auntie, please stop singing!"

"You're disgusting trying to play innocent! You think I don't know what you were doing meeting with him at the church all the time? Following him to every event; every preaching engagement; every teaching opportunity he had? You think I don't know what your infatuation with my husband turned into? You disgust me! You couldn't just be satisfied with his attention like the others. YOU had to be at the center." Lady Lorna looked like a crazed woman now. She was literally spitting words out at Tilda.

"Your iniquities manifested into this bastard child, and he didn't want you anymore. That's when you decided to shut him up and tell lies!!" Her hair had come out of the pinned up-do she had come to the table wearing making her appear completely disheveled.

By this time, Vicki was piling food on multiple plates and stuffing rolls in her purse.

"Well, Caring, this was so nice. Dinner was good, Girl, but we got to go. I forgot I got to, uhhhhh. I got to, ummmm...Girl, I got a man", she paused briefly and looked at

Carrington.

"Girl, I got a man, and he's handicapped. Yeah, and I forgot to charge up his motorized wheelchair, so I got to get back home so he ain't crawling all over the floor! He texted me that he had fallen, and he's stuck. Come on, Tilda. Caring, go get our coats." Vicki started trying to pull Tilda from her seat.

Carrington turned to look at her aunt. She couldn't believe how horrible a liar her auntie had become. "What!?"

"Yeah, Girl. You know I'm new at this, but he's sweet so I decided not to discrimage against him." Vicki just wanted to get Tilda out of the house before she said something that she would regret. She knew this was not how Tilda wanted to tell Caring about her father.

"Discriminate? Is that what you mean, Auntie?" Carrington was just going to go with Vicki's lie because of the fear of what was about to come out of her mother's mouth.

"I wish I had killed him." Tilda's entire body was visibly shaking.

The room went silent. James was flabbergasted by her words. Tears began to run down Tilda's face. She was gripping the table cloth.

"You are accusing me of an affair with YOUR husband? I was a child. I looked up to him to teach what God had not yet given me an understanding of in His Word. I was a child who just wanted to learn. I was A CHILD who wanted to understand her calling. I was A CHILD YOUR HUSBAND RAPED, and you are just as sick as he was!!!"

"He was sick, but YOU took full advantage of his bad habits, didn't you?!"

"YOU are SICK!!! You knew what he was doing, and you said nothing? It was easier for you to accuse those other women than to confront your husband!" Tilda was screaming and crying. "YOU could have saved me!!!"

Carrington felt sick to her stomach. She was a product of rape. Her head began to spin. She began to look around the room for someone with sanity that could help her understand. She saw Leigha shaking her bowed head, and Jacob with his head lifted toward the ceiling as if praying.

Before she could gather her thoughts enough to say something, James had already asked the question.

"My father was a womanizer, child molester, and rapist?" James sat back in his chair so hard it rocked as if someone had knocked him backward. "Wait! Carrington is my sister? Mother, please. Please, tell me you didn't know any of this. Please, tell me Minister Tilda is lying!" James was begging like a little child.

"Shut up, James! Don't you see what she has done? She killed your father and broke our family! It is only fair that she be exposed, and endure the same pain. She needs to know what it feels like to have your family ripped apart. Now, it's done! I'm ready to go to my room."

"You're not going anywhere, Lorna. What have you done, Sister?" Leigha stood up and approached her sister. "It's time to face the truth and get real help, Lorna." Jacob was right behind her.

Tilda stood at the end of the table sobbing as she looked at Carrington who refused to look back at her. The pain she saw coming from her only child was killing her.

"Lorna, you are angry at Daddy, and you have deflected that anger on everyone except him. DADDY RAPED ME, LORNA! I didn't break up our family; Daddy's sick ways broke up our family. I know you loved him, and you didn't know any better than to ignore his faults. Ignoring mental instability doesn't make it disappear. After I was raped, Mother realized that, and she had to do something so she made him leave." Leigha reached out to her sister. "You married a man that reminded you of the man you felt you lost. Lorna, please, it's time to get help. It's time to heal."

Lorna stood up from the table without a word or glance at her sister.

"Carrington," Tilda barely spoke above a whisper, "Carrington, please look at me."

"Me-ma. It was Me-ma. It wasn't you," Carrington looked into her mother's pain-stricken face. "It was Me-ma. She killed my father because he raped you. That's why she asked me to forgive her the night she died."

"Yes, Caring." Tilda suddenly felt so tired.

Vicki had escaped the table and moved faster than she ever had repacking the car. She appeared at Tilda's side with her coat. "Come on, Tilda, we need to get you outta here before you get a charge, and I get that third strike." She glared at Lorna who stood like a cold statue with hatred shooting from her eyes like darts.

"James, my grandmother murdered your father, I mean our father, out of rage and hurt. I'm the product of the rape he committed." Carrington turned back to her mother who sat defeated beside her. She reached for her mother's hand. "I'm the product of my mother's pain.

"I'm so sorry you had to find out this way, Carrington." Tilda didn't know what else to say. She wished she had listened to Pastor when he told her to tell Caring.

"Caring, you may have been the result of an extremely malicious act, but from the moment I held you in my arms, you became the light that rose out of the darkness. You are living evidence of how God works all things together for the good of those who love Him and whom He has called according to His purpose." Looking into her daughter's tear-stained face she spoke, "A portion of His love for me is what came from my womb. Watching that love grow every day is what helped me to move forward and heal."

James stood from his seat. He had heard Tilda's emotional plea to her daughter and could see no reason to carry any hate toward her. She was a scared child and had no control over her own mother's reaction. He could see himself doing the same for his own child. He stood to leave the dining room.

"James!" He turned to see his uncle step in his direction. As the truth of Tilda's past came to light, his mother rested her head on her sister's shoulder and began crying. She, herself, looked like a scared little girl.

As his aunt rocked, he could hear his mother whimpering, "Why, Daddy? Why?" It was more than he could bear. He was so angry with her, but anyone could tell this woman was not well.

"Jacob, not now." Leigha looked up at Jacob with a longing gaze.

"Don't, Jacob. Please, no. Don't break my family more than we have already been broken." Lorna continued to sob.

"When then, Lorna? Answer me. Leigha? We have skated around the truth and lied to this boy since he was a child!! We've been lying to ourselves."

Seeing her husband's pain, Leigha knew that any response James gave would only cause more anguish. Silently pleading with the love of her life, Leigha allowed her own tears to flow. Jacob, once again, conceded to the sisters' wishes.

"Go. Take some time by yourself. We'll talk later after we take care of your mother." James knew this was not what Jacob wanted to say, but he accepted it just so he could escape the room.

After Jacob and Leigha left with Lorna, Carrington asked Vicki to take her mother to the car and wait for her. She tried to appear strong in front of her mother, but her heart was breaking once again. She had fallen in love with her own brother for a second time. She instructed the kitchen staff on what to do after they were done cleaning, and then she went to her room to gather her still packed bags. Even after she decided to stay with James, she didn't bother to unpack. Carrington did not want to just leave him alone without saying good-bye; after all, he was her brother. She found him in his study sitting in his office chair staring out of the window at the lake.

"James? May I come in?" Carrington did not know where his mind was and dared not enter without his permission.

"Yes."

"I just came to say I'm not angry at your mother. I know everyone has a thousand thoughts, but this is that key we talked about. Better days are coming, James. Please, don't give up on God or your calling." Carrington sincerely meant every word she spoke to him.

He knew she meant well, but the pain made it all hard to receive at the moment. He did manage to speak, "Thank you, Carrington."

"But until then, James, I think we need to file for divorce as soon as possible. I don't want anything so it should not be a problem." Carrington felt a lump in her throat.

He did not move or speak a word for what seemed to be an eternity. Then, "I have already called the lawyer. The papers are being drawn up as we speak."

There was very little emotion in his words, and he refused to look at her.

"I will have them mailed to Pastor Tilda's home. You probably should go, now, Carrington." He hated dismissing her this way, but if she stayed any longer he would not be able to see her for whom she really was now. She was his little sister.

Without a word, and with silent tears streaming, Carrington left the place she had just become comfortable with calling home. She found her mother in the backseat of the car waiting for her. Tilda held her baby girl all the way back to Alabama as Carrington cried herself to sleep.

Chapter 15
Carrington
After the Storm

After that weekend of reckoning, Lorna was placed in a mental health facility that specialized in counseling residents and not just medicating them. She fought them with everything she had initially, but after firing all of her lawyers in a fit of unprovoked rage and hurting herself in the courtroom, the Judge decided it was in her best interest to receive help. Leigha had explained to Carrington that the facility was only thirty minutes away from her home, and she was able to visit and have family counseling with her sister three times a week. Leigha updated James and Carrington on Lorna's progress weekly and reported that she was doing better than she had ever seen. Despite the deceit and pain, Lorna had caused, Carrington was so glad to hear of her healing process and progress.

It took a while, but James finally started working on his own healing. He started seeing a counselor to work through his anger with his mother. Then, he joined family counseling with his aunt, uncle, and mother. It was during one of their sessions that he found out that James C. Hewman was not his father after all. His mother admitted that during one of her spirals, she had successfully seduced her brother-in-law who was having marital issues with her sister. This one time resulted in James's conception. She wanted to hurt Leigha, and break up her family liked she chose to believe Leigha had done to their family. When she realized she was pregnant, Lorna tried to hide it from everyone by saying it was her husband's baby, but Jacob had confessed everything to Leigha to mend his own family. They went along with Lorna's schemes so she wouldn't ruin Jacob's new pastorship. Even though James was in disbelief, he was relieved that he and Carrington were not siblings. He was in love with her; truly in love. Shortly after Hewman's murder, Lorna finally broke and had to be committed. James was given to Jacob and Leigha right after his birth. Jacob and Leigha explained everything to Silas

after James was told about his true
conception.

Carrington was not his sister! James
was angry that it had taken so long for his
mother and aunt to tell him this, but
continuing with therapy helped him to have
compassion and eventually forgive, both,
them and his biological father, Jacob. That
void that he had of not knowing his father
became filled as he realized his father had
always been right there in his life. Even if he
didn't know it then, James was blessed to
have Jacob in his life. It was Jacob that drove
with him to Alabama to go get his wife. This
time, James handled things the respectful
way.

Without Carrington knowing, James
and Jacob called and explained things to
Tilda and Pastor. James and Carrington's
parents spoke for hours as he updated them
on his mother and the rest of the family.
James asked Pastor and Tilda for
Carrington's hand in marriage. This time all
was well in Tilda's heart, and by the next
morning, Jacob and James were on the road.

Upon their arrival, Pastor and Tilda met them outside with a warm welcome. James did not even want any food; he wanted Carrington. Tilda placed her hands on his cheeks, "Son, go get your wife." James didn't have to say thank you. He hugged Tilda so tightly that she was out of breath by the time he let go.

James entered Carrington's room without knocking and scooped her up from her bed.

"James, what are you doing here? Put me down!" Carrington looked at him like he was crazy. She was terrified of her mother finding him there.

"Carrington, you are not my sister." Before she could utter one question, he kissed her with a new passion. "You are my wife, and I'm taking you home."

Once, again, Caring packed her belongings, but this time her mother was at her side to help. She knew God had kept His Word and things were on the right track. Saying there "see you laters", Carrington headed back to Michigan with James and Jacob. There was not a cloud of darkness in sight.

Leigha was glad that Carrington did not hesitate to return with James and so was Carrington. Regardless of how they started, as time passed James showed more of himself to her. They had also started pre-marital counseling and were healing. They had long conversations and leaned on the Lord and one another. They studied and prayed together. The healing was still taking place, but Carrington was smiling again. She and James were friends. It had taken a while, but there was more blossoming between them. There was an attraction that was more than physical. Tilda and Pastor Lugi prayed with the young couple often. Things had indeed changed.

On what would have been their eighth anniversary, James and Carrington remarried. That night they consummated their nuptials as she had always dreamed. It was an experience that was well worth waiting for, and James made sure that it was one Carrington would never forget. It was her very first time. In the words of the Great Betty Wright, it was the night he made her a woman.

James proved himself to be a holy husband and even shared his testimony with the new church that had called him to pastor: Gracious Beginnings Christian Church. He shared with them that they needed to know his story so that they understood why he would only accept the position if they accepted his wife as their Co-Pastor. They posed no arguments. That Christmas, with many family members in attendance, James and Carrington were officially installed.

After service and dinner, James expressed his need to see Lorna. He asked his wife; his brother and his family; and their parents to escort him to see his mother. The love that was continuously growing between them led them to agree that the wonderful news of his new position should be shared with her.

Arriving at the care facility, the family gathered in the beautifully decorated private family room. A nurse escorted a refreshed-looking Lorna into the room and left her with her family. Lorna sat beside James and received hugs from everyone. She stood when Tilda approached and hugged her the longest. From the trembling of Tilda's shoulders, everyone knew she was crying. No one could hear what Lorna whispered, but it could be seen to have blessed both women.

"How are you, Mother?" James held her hand as she took her seat.

"I am healthy in body, mind, and spirit, Son. I'm blessed to see my family loves me still and has come to visit me." Lorna looked at all of their faces with so much gratitude for God's forgiveness.

"Mother, we came to tell you that I have been installed at a church not far from here: Gracious Beginnings Christian Church. Carrington and I are moving closer to Mama Leigha, Dad, and you."

Leigha took James in another embrace. "I'm so happy for you, Son. You will do especially well with that angel by your side." She looked at Carrington.

"Thank you for not holding my transgressions against my son, Carrington. The very people I have tried to hurt have blessed me with what I have always longed for: the perfect family." She looked at each and every one of them with a sincere expression of love and thankfulness.

Carrington stood up from her seat on the other side of James and went to Lorna's side. James still clutched one of his mother's hands. Taking her free hand, Carrington placed it on the growing bulge in her belly.

"No, Mother Lorna, we are not perfect, but we do serve a wonderfully perfect God who has given us, yet, another reason to forgive and love one another."

With tears streaming down her face, Lorna, looked into Carrington's glowing face. She knew that finally a seed had been planted in good ground, and God would soon grace them with an extraordinary harvest.

About Author

Dr. Tamara S. La Guins had a tumultuous start in life, but through ex those traumatic experiences, God became a her close friend. She credits her journey with fueling her dreams of becoming best-selling author and actress and answering to the call of evangelism and service to God's people. Believing knowledge is power, she has degrees in Counseling and Divinity. Dr. La Guins is a mentor and spiritual leader for those who are broken, afraid, and angry because of their past or present situations and circumstances, and is continues to work in the field of Education.

She lives in Georgia with her husband, children, and dog; all she describes as her grace-given blessings. If she is remembered for nothing else, she wants to be remembered as a Child of God.

Reaping What You Sow